SU

As the surge_____ _____
their eyes m_____ _____
head-on with _____ _____
the blaze _____ _____ beautiful eyes
threatened to melt the ice that he had
packed about his heart to protect himself from her insidious appeal. An almost
tender amusement struggled with his
irritation—and lost.

'Your nurses lack discipline, Sister,'
he said brusquely, knowing that the
efficiency of the unit was her pride. 'A
month at Benedict's would do most of
them a great deal of good!'

'Even Benedict's nurses must drop
things on occasions,' Lucilla returned
pleasantly, knowing he was being deliberately offensive and refusing to be drawn
into open argument. She'd met arrogant
surgeons before, many of them. It was her
first experience of one who seemed so
determined to be disliked!

Lynne Collins has written twenty-four Doctor Nurse Romances based on personal experience of hospital life backed by research and information from her many friends in the medical profession. She likes writing about hospital settings, with their wealth of human interest. Married with one son and now living on the Essex coast, Lynne enjoys travel, meeting people, talking, walking and gardening. She has also written several Doctor Nurse Romances under the pen-name of Lindsay Hicks.

SURGEON AT BAY

BY

LYNNE COLLINS

MILLS & BOON LIMITED
ETON HOUSE 18–24 PARADISE ROAD
RICHMOND SURREY TW9 1SR

First published in Great Britain 1987
by Mills & Boon Limited

© Lynne Collins 1987

Australian copyright 1987
Philippine copyright 1987

ISBN 0 263 75879 6

Set in 10 on 11 pt Linotron Times
03–1087–57,350

Photoset by Rowland Phototypesetting Limited
Bury St Edmunds, Suffolk
Made and printed in Great Britain by
William Collins Sons & Co Limited, Glasgow

CHAPTER ONE

CARRYING out her usual early-morning tour of inspection, Lucilla left the scrub annexe of an operating theatre to make her way along a deceptively quiet corridor. The surgeons hadn't yet arrived to scrub up and the first patient still had to be sent up from the wards. But the theatre unit of the Camhurst General Hospital was a hive of activity behind the scenes.

The slender girl in the thin green dress, red-gold curls crammed into a regulation mob cap and looking much too young for her responsible job, received only an indifferent glance from the man who thrust through the swing doors of the unit as she approached. Tall, broad-shouldered and strikingly handsome with dark hair and eyes and bronzed good looks, he strode towards her with an air of arrogant approval of his surroundings, and Lucilla frowned, wondering who he was and what he wanted. The frown deepened as the stranger paused to throw open the door of a clinical room and glance in with obvious interest.

It wasn't unknown for patient or visitor to lose themselves in the maze of corridors and departments of the big hospital and wander by chance into the antiseptic realms of Theatres, and it was part of Lucilla's job to intercept intruders and shoo them out before a sterile area could be invaded or a surgeon interrupted in the middle of delicate surgery.

But there was something about this particular intruder that made her uneasy. There had recently been a spate of thefts of drugs and medical supplies from other hospitals in the district, and the staff had been warned to be on the alert for suspicious characters wandering about where they had no business to be.

He didn't look like a suspicious character, she admitted. In fact, he looked more like eminent doctor or surgeon in the well-cut grey suit and with his well-groomed appearance and that distinctive air of authority that was familiar to any trained nurse. Lucilla really had no good reason for her distrust of him except an odd prickle of apprehension at the nape of her neck, as though all her instincts were sending out alarm signals.

But that very impressive appearance and attitude would be a valuable asset if he *was* a thief who specialised in stealing from hospitals. For, wearing the white coat of doctor or surgeon, he could probably walk in and out of any ward or department and help himself to various items without arousing the least suspicion. Although, at the same time, he would surely be remarked and remembered for that distinctive height and the good looks that must cause a few feminine hearts to flutter.

He seemed to be defying her or anyone else to challenge him as he strolled through the unit in that self-assured manner. Without hesitation and with a determined glint in her grey eyes, Lucilla stepped into his path.

'Can I help you?' she suggested with a bright, professional smile and the brisk, businesslike manner that she had been forced to cultivate to overcome the dual drawback of youth and extreme prettiness, tired of not being taken seriously. It had proved very useful when dealing with difficult patients or rebellious junior nurses or bumptious housemen.

Pausing, he looked down his very handsome nose at her, visibly unimpressed. 'No, thank you, Nurse. I don't need your assistance,' he assured her dismissively.

The rich throb of his deep voice seemed to strike some

chord of response in her slight frame. But she was instantly and unreasonably irritated by his attitude and her chin tilted.

'That depends on what you want, doesn't it?' she countered with a touch of hauteur. 'Unless you have some authority to be in this part of the hospital, I'm afraid I must ask you to leave.'

There was the hint of outrage in the lift of a curving dark brow. 'Must you? Why?'

'I've just told you. Only members of staff are allowed to enter Theatres.'

'No problem, then. I *am* staff.' He attempted to brush past, impatient, autocratic.

Lucilla didn't believe him. It was too prompt and too glib, and she suspected that he was trying to bluff his way out of an awkward situation. Maybe it had been successful strategy in the past, but she hoped she wasn't so easily gulled by someone who claimed to be on the staff but appeared to be totally ignorant of her identity and status.

Stubbornly, she blocked his path. 'You can prove that, I suppose?' Her manner was pleasant, but there was an unmistakable challenge behind the words.

Annoyance sparked in the dark eyes that were set deep in the lean, attractive face. 'I'm not aware of the necessity to prove anything to you, Nurse!' he snapped.

'Perhaps you'd prefer to prove it to Security?' Lucilla suggested crisply.

He glowered, mobile mouth tightening. 'Call Security, by all means. We shall see which of us is red-faced as a result!'

Doubt flickered then, but she stood her ground. 'If you *are* staff then I'll apologise, of course—as soon as I've seen some proof of your identity. And if you can provide it then you ought not to mind being asked,' she added reasonably.

His anger exploded. 'This is intolerable! How dare you question me just because I'm not wearing greens or a name-badge? Is Sister on duty? I'll have a word with her and see if she encourages her nurses to behave like members of the KGB!'

Lucilla wasn't impressed by the show of righteous indignation, but she realised that it would probably awe a junior nurse into believing that she'd offended someone of importance in the hospital hierarchy. She wasn't a junior, however. She wasn't awed by the anger or the arrogance of a man who ought to be well aware that she wasn't just another nurse if he was really a member of the staff.

'If you have a complaint, make it to me,' she said coolly. 'I'm Sister Theatres.'

His eyes narrowed abruptly. 'You can prove that, I suppose?' He deliberately echoed her challenge, partly to annoy, partly to give himself time to assimilate the unexpected announcement of her identity.

Lucilla's chin flew up. 'Of course! If necessary.' Theatre greens might turn her into a seemingly anonymous member of the theatre staff, but it would be a simple matter to produce her staff pass if he insisted. 'But you may safely take my word for it that I'm Lucilla Flint.'

He looked her over with a curl to his lip. 'Then you surely should know a surgeon when you see one, Sister,' he said with biting sarcasm.

'Surgeons come in all shapes and sizes and seldom have two heads,' she retorted tartly. 'Usually they have excellent manners too—but there has to be an exception to every rule, apparently!'

He scowled. 'If I'd known I'd have you to deal with I'd have turned down the job of Senior Surgical Officer,' he declared bluntly.

Lucilla stared at the words, the warmth of dismay

flooding into her delicately pretty face. 'You're Paul Savidge,' she said stiffly, in belated realisation, annoyed that she had failed to connect the glowing verbal descriptions of the newly appointed SSO with this tall, dark and much too good-looking man who had arrived days earlier than expected.

'A gleam of intelligence, thank God!' he said nastily.

She stiffened. She might have alienated him by not recognising his right to stride through Theatres as though he owned the entire hospital, but that didn't entitle him to be rude to her. She'd met arrogant surgeons before, many of them. It was her first experience of one who seemed so determined to be disliked!

It wasn't the best beginning to working together in the coming months. Lucilla knew she must make an effort to overcome the animosity emanating from the surgeon, if only for the sake of her Sister's badge. Just now, she was close to slapping his handsome face!

'We didn't meet when you came to look round, did we? I was off duty that day. So it isn't surprising that we didn't recognise each other.' The crisp words neatly apportioned the blame for the misunderstanding between them both, although she privately felt that a less arrogant man would have announced his identity right away and not allowed her to blunder into near-accusation and end up feeling foolish. Mustering a smile, she held out her hand. 'Welcome to the General, anyway . . .'

'Thank you.' It was cold, unbending, and he ignored the warm friendliness of that sudden smile and her outstretched hand. They might have to work together, but he wasn't prepared to accept her as a new friend, Paul Savidge thought harshly.

Feeling chilled, puzzled by the apparent enmity in his manner, Lucilla let her hand fall. There wasn't even the glimmer of a smile in the dark eyes that looked so coldly and yet so compellingly into her own. A sudden shiver swept the length of her spine and the hair on the back of her neck prickled all over again as she saw a blaze in the depths of those eyes, a smouldering fire beneath the ice that set her tingling.

She experienced a confusion of emotions, a strange excitement that shocked her senses to an awareness of his very potent masculinity and an even stranger conviction that his advent presented some kind of threat. It was a cataclysmic rush of feeling, totally without rhyme or reason to it, like nothing she'd ever known before. In that brief, startled moment when she looked into the glinting dark eyes of a stranger, she felt that her life would never be the same again now that Paul Savidge had walked into it.

She didn't like him at all. A primitive fear of him stirred, deep down, difficult to analyse. But he was the most attractive man she had ever met, and something quickened to life in the very depths of her being as their eyes locked . . .

She pulled herself together hastily. The junior nurses might be fascinated by his good looks and physical magnetism, but she had better things to do than waste time and energy on fancying the new SSO!

'We didn't expect you until next week,' she said, not caring that it sounded like a rebuke. It *was* a rebuke. Advance warning of his arrival that morning might have armed her for his arrogance and scornful attitude.

'I decided to spend a day or two getting to know the place and the people and finding out how the unit is run. You don't object, I hope, Sister?' His tone implied that any objection she ventured to make would be brushed aside as irrelevant.

'An excellent idea,' Lucilla approved. 'You'd better come along to my office and I'll give you some coffee and do my best to answer some of your questions while things are quiet.'

He looked up and down the silent corridor with a frown that harshened his handsome features. 'Things seem exceptionally quiet, Sister. The place appears to be deserted, in fact. Isn't anyone here yet?'

Lucilla bridled. By '*anyone*', he was probably referring to surgeons like himself. Someone of real importance, in his view! She doubted if hard-working nurses and technicians counted in his arrogant estimation. Any more than *she* did! It was obvious that he didn't like her and wasn't impressed by her. Fortunately, she ran the unit well enough to please the hospital authorities and she didn't have to worry about pleasing a surgeon with an exaggerated idea of his own importance! On or off duty! Away from the General, there was no reason why she should even have to meet Paul Savidge, she thought thankfully. There was nothing in her contract that stipulated that she had to be on friendly terms with the SSO!

'Some of the staff are getting the theatres ready for the morning lists. The surgeons will start to arrive shortly. I believe you know Evan Pritchard? He's doing a Caesarean section this morning—and here comes the anaesthetist who usually works with him,' she added as a green-clad figure came into view at the end of the corridor. 'I think you must have met Laurie Jesmond . . . ?'

She welcomed the approaching anaesthetist with a warm smile, feeling that his light touch might dispel the tension in the atmosphere that wasn't entirely due to the fact that she and the new SSO had started off on the wrong foot.

'Savidge! How are you? We didn't hope to see you so soon,' Laurie exclaimed with every appearance of genuine delight, shaking hands with the surgeon. 'Come to put us through our paces and find out how we shape, have you? Excellent! Some of us shape better than others, of course—as no doubt you've already noticed,' he added with a mischievous glance in Lucilla's direction.

The implied compliment brought a dawning blush to her cheeks and the hint of a smile, for she was fond of the irrepressible young doctor. But she reproved him with a sharp look, convinced that the new SSO was unlikely to approve of the informal friendliness that made life easier for everyone who worked in Theatres.

'Good morning, Mr Jesmond,' she said in her best Sister-Starch manner, hoping that Laurie would take the hint and refrain from flirting with her nurses and herself in his usual lighthearted fashion that morning.

'Sister Flint!' he exclaimed incorrigibly, pretending to be astonished, bowing low. 'Why, 'tis yourself, to be sure! And here's me thinking 'tis a fairy princess come to see us, so fresh and lovely as you look.' The light words in a mock-Irish accent tripped easily from his tongue, but there was genuine admiration and affection in his bright blue eyes. Ignoring her warning glance, he put an arm about her waist. 'And how *is* my best girl this morning?' he added warmly.

Lucilla drew away, frowning, conscious of scathing disapproval in a pair of watching dark eyes. 'Much too busy for your nonsense,' she said crisply, wishing Laurie a hundred miles away and hoping the surgeon hadn't been misled into supposing they were more than friends. Even if it wasn't any of his business!

As if to underline her words, a flustered nurse appeared in the doorway of a nearby clinical room. 'Do come and have a look at this autoclave, Sister! I think it's about to blow up!'

Lucilla couldn't ignore the anguished appeal, although she knew it was an exaggeration. The sterilising equipment was temperamental at times but perfectly safe.

'Very well, Nurse. I'll be there in a moment.' She turned to Laurie. 'Would you look after Mr Savidge? I promised him some coffee . . .'

'Sure. No problem,' he responded promptly.

Lucilla hurried to the clinical room to deal with the autoclave, thankful to be relieved of responsibility for the SSO. For there was still much to be done before the rush of arriving surgeons and prepped patients began the day in earnest.

Paul Savidge looked after her with intent, narrowed eyes, his expression giving nothing away while, inside him, was a tightly coiled spring of anger.

Misinterpreting the look in his eyes, Laurie grinned. 'Terrific girl, isn't she?' he enthused, feeling that no man could be immune to the attractions of the pretty Theatre Sister. 'Makes a change from some of the hatchet-faced nurses we have to work with at times, doesn't it? She's a really nice girl as well as being great at her job. She gets on well with everyone and brightens up the place just by being around. I don't know what we'd do without our Lucy.'

'Quite an accolade,' Paul said coldly. 'But she only needs to be good at her job to suit me—and I prefer to make up my own mind about that.'

Even the exuberant Laurie felt crushed by the chilly rejoinder. Wondering how Lucilla had managed to offend the man within minutes of meeting him, he leaped rather too quickly to her defence.

'Oh, sure!' he shrugged. 'No need to take my word for it. Lucilla and I are very good friends and I daresay I'm biased in her favour. She'll be scrubbing for Evan Pritchard this morning, as usual. Friend of yours, isn't he? There's your chance to see a really good team in action.'

Paul was no longer listening with more than half an ear, having dismissed the subject of Lucilla Flint, more intent on learning the layout of the unit as he was led along corridors to the sitting-room where the surgeons usually congregated between operations to drink coffee and talk shop.

He was impatient with Jesmond's too obvious liking for the girl and the admiration that no doubt extended far beyond her qualities as a nurse. Knowing what he did about Lucilla Flint, he wasn't prepared to take more than a professional interest in someone who might or might not be good at her job but was certainly hopeless at hiding an immediate response to a man's physical attractions.

Paul had recognised a too-familiar flutter of excited reaction to his good looks and powerful physique and observed the spark of interest and feminine calculation in those wide grey eyes, and he despised her for it.

He had excellent reason for ensuring that he had no more to do with Lucilla Flint than his new job demanded. When he had heard that the post of Senior Surgical Officer at the Camhurst General was up for grabs, at a time when he had personal reasons for wanting to get away from London, he had had no idea that she worked at the same hospital as Sister Theatres. It was not until he had been appointed as SSO that a casual remark had alerted him to the fact that he would be working with someone whose very name could stir him to feelings of anger and contempt.

He had never met Lucilla Flint, but he had heard a lot about her, none of it to her credit. Now that they had met, Paul conceded that she was a very good-looking girl. In any other circumstances, he might have found her attractive. As it was, he was wholly immune to the feminine charms that had already caused so much havoc and heartache. Forwarned was forearmed, and it would take a lot more than Lucilla Flint's pretty face and golden smile and shapely body to penetrate the armour of his dislike.

Having dealt summarily with the temperamental steril-iser, Lucilla continued on her way to the theatre that was being prepared for Evan Pritchard's use by a team of nurses under the supervision of a staff nurse who was friend and former flatmate. She wasn't at all surprised to discover that the new SSO was the main topic of conversation as the nurses worked.

'I shall be sick of the sound of the man's name by the end of the day,' she confided ruefully to Julie, who had shared her training days and later encouraged her to apply for the job of Theatre Sister at the Camhurst General.

Julie looked up from the tray of instruments. 'New faces are bound to be talked about. But I did warn you that he would be a disturbing influence on our impressionable young.'

Lucilla was rather more concerned with Paul Savidge's disturbing influence on her own emotions as she remembered the tilt of her heart and the alarming stir of her senses.

'He's very attractive,' she conceded, careful not to sound too unimpressed or too approving, knowing her friend's romantic tendencies.

'And knows it,' Julie deplored unexpectedly. 'He seems thoroughly spoiled, don't you think? The type who'd consider himself the answer to a maiden's prayer —if he deigned to notice her in the first place.'

'I didn't get the impression that you weren't impressed when you were going on about him at length the other day,' teased Lucilla, slightly surprised.

'As a married woman, I'm doing my best to resist his vibes—and that isn't easy! I suppose *you* didn't even

notice that he had any! I bet your cautious heart didn't
miss a single beat when he walked in!'

Lucilla was thankful that her friend didn't know just
how oddly her usually cautious heart had behaved that
morning.

'To be honest, I thought he was after our drugs. Not
having met him and not expecting him to turn up un-
announced, I leaped to the conclusion that he was the
fellow who's been doing the thieving. Unfortunately, I
made it obvious that I suspected him of being up to no
good, which rather dented his dignity and didn't endear
me at all.' She smiled ruefully. 'He was so beastly about
it that I wasn't at all inclined to lose my heart to him.'

'If you still have it to lose,' Julie suggested with a
sly twinkle. 'A little bird told me that you and Evan
Pritchard were getting on very well at Brendan's party
the other night.'

'One rubs shoulders with a lot of people at parties,'
Lucilla reminded her airily. 'One drink too many and
some of them say and do things they prefer to forget the
next morning. I've known Evan too long to believe that
he really fancies me. I just happened to be the only
unattached female at that party, that's all.'

She'd been pleased when the good-looking gynae
surgeon gravitated to her side and stayed there, but she
hadn't attached much importance to his show of interest.
He had a reputation for light loving and she had been
careful not to encourage him in the year that they'd
known each other since she came to Camhurst. She had
left the party before Evan could suggest taking her home
at the end of it, suspecting what he had in mind to round
off the evening. She knew that Evan liked her. She liked
him too. But she didn't want to be listed as one of his
many girl-friends.

Satisfied that the theatre was ready for use, she went
away to inspect the others and to find jobs for two

juniors who seemed to have nothing better to do than gossip in a scrub annexe.

As Sister Theatres, Lucilla was very conscious of her responsibilities. The Camhurst General Hospital took patients from a wide catchment area and dealt with all the accident and emergency cases in the area. The four theatres were in constant use and she prided herself on coping without fuss, organising staff and facilities to meet every eventuality. She was determined that no one should ever be able to say she was too young or too inexperienced for her very demanding job.

She knew that she looked younger than her twenty-five years and that she wasn't always taken seriously at first by new members of the staff. But they quickly learned to respect her efficiency and to disregard the youthful, fragile prettiness that had always been something of a handicap to a dedicated nurse. Usually they soon learned to like her too.

Lucille hoped the new SSO wouldn't prove to be an exception on every score.

CHAPTER TWO

LUCILLA was speaking to the Sister in charge of the Maternity Unit when Evan Pritchard entered her office, big and blond and good-looking, much admired and sighed over by the junior nurses and one of the nicest men she knew.

She nodded to him. 'Mrs Wells is on her way,' she announced, replacing the receiver.

'Good. I'm just going to scrub. I hope you're free to assist me?' he asked with a flash of his attractive smile.

'I daresay that can be arranged.' Her own smile was warm but slightly conscious as she recalled the way she'd run out on him at Brendan's party. She hadn't seen Evan since that evening and she half expected him to make some reproachful comment.

'You're the best we've got, you know—I've just been saying so to Savidge. You know he's turned up this morning, I suppose? Testing the water before he dives in head-first.'

'Yes. We met when he arrived.' Lucilla tried to sound as if the encounter hadn't etched itself indelibly on her mind. Feeling her face grow warm at the memory, she picked up a file and turned away to restore it to a cabinet.

'He's decided to get into greens and give a hand with my section. I've given you a glowing reference, so I shall be relying on you to live up to it,' Evan warned her teasingly.

She wrinkled her nose at him with a rueful laugh. 'Thanks! I shall be all fingers and thumbs now!' She wished he hadn't sung her praises to someone who

probably had no desire to hear them, no doubt prefer-
ring to decide for himself if her work matched the high
standards of Benedict's Theatre Sisters.

'You'll be fine,' Evan promised.

Lucilla hesitated. 'You knew Paul Savidge when you
were at Benedict's, didn't you?'

'In the distant days of my youth.'

'He's about your age, isn't he? Were you medical
students together?'

'That's right. He was an arrogant devil with a critical
attitude and a tongue to match in those days, and I don't
suppose he's changed very much. We haven't met in
years, but if he's only half as good at his job as he's
reputed to be then we're very lucky to get him,' said
Evan generously.

'He's rumoured to be quite brilliant.'

'He was on the short list for a consultancy at
Benedict's, but opted out for personal reasons, I gather.'

Lucilla longed to know more, but she didn't want
Evan or anyone else to suspect the extent of her interest
in Paul Savidge. She was still trying to convince herself
that it was a very natural interest in a newcomer.

Rather abruptly, she changed the subject. 'Tell me
about Mrs Wells. What's the actual problem?'

'As you know, she's thirty-eight and a primipara, and
she's had problems throughout her pregnancy.'

'Very late to be having a first baby,' Lucilla com-
mented.

'Yes. The baby's on the big side too. She's a very
determined lady who's spent a lot of money on private
treatment in order to have a child, and it's very important to her that nothing should go wrong now. I mean to
see that it doesn't,' he said firmly.

The trundle of a trolley's wheels in the corridor
announced the arrival of the patient. Mrs Wells was
whisked into an ante-room where Laurie waited with a

hypodermic syringe at the ready.

Surgeon and Theatre Sister went along to the scrub
annexe to don gowns and masks. Evan wondered if
Lucilla was avoiding personalities as she continued to
talk about the patient and the proposed surgery. She
had always kept him at a slight, discouraging distance
until the other evening when they had met at Brendan's
party and he had set out to reassure her about his
much-exaggerated reputation as a Casanova. Relaxed,
friendly and more communicative than usual, Lucilla
had been good company, and he had enjoyed the evening and begun to be optimistic about their future
relationship. So he had been disappointed when she said
her good nights and slipped away while his back was
briefly turned.

'You don't seem to be your usual unruffled self this
morning,' he ventured as they stood side by side at the
basins, scrubbing hands and nails with practised thor-
oughness. 'Did I do or say something you didn't like the
other evening? Is that why you left the party in such a
rush?'

'No, of course not. I had a lovely time.' Lucilla skated
over her reason for that abrupt departure. 'Do I seem
fraught? I've a lot on my mind this morning. It's going to
be a hectic day even if we're spared any extra cases
coming up from A & E.'

'Then you'll need to relax at the end of it,' Evan said
promptly. 'How about having a drink with me—
and maybe a meal if you've no other plans for the
evening?'

She hesitated, not wanting to seem too eager to accept
a casual invitation at short notice. 'We'll see,' she compromised. 'I might be dead on my feet by the end of the
day.' She issued the light warning, but she smiled at him
in a way that held the hint of a promise. For she did like
Evan, and it might be more sensible to encourage his

interest than to hanker for a man who seemed to have
made up his mind to dislike her on sight, she told herself
sensibly.

Entering, Paul Savidge saw the dazzle of that golden
smile for his friend and felt a flicker of irritation. Someone so distractingly pretty ought not to be allowed within
miles of an operating theatre, he thought impatiently.
He wasn't easily distracted, but a less disciplined man
might be, and it was essential for a surgeon to keep his
mind on his work.

Turning, Lucilla saw the surgeon, broad shoulders
straining the seams of his thin green tunic, crisp black
curls scarcely covered by the theatre cap and his mask
dangling by its tapes about his neck. The deep V of the
tunic revealed the bronzed column of his throat and
hinted at the powerful chest with its tangle of curling
black hair. Unexpectedly, her senses quickened and she
melted with a longing that was in strange and startling
contrast to the dislike and resentment that he'd triggered
off at that first encounter.

She meant to smile, to say something warm and
welcoming, for she didn't want to be on bad terms with
the new SSO. But the chill in the dark eyes as they skated
over her froze both the smile and the friendly words that
hovered on her lips.

Striding to a basin beside Evan, he turned on the tap
and began to scrub hands and strong forearms beneath
the running water.

'I hear that there's an excellent golf club in Camhurst
and that you're a member. I'm relying on you to intro-
duce me to the club secretary. Maybe we can have a
round this weekend . . .?'

It was unreasonable to feel that he deliberately ex-
cluded her as he spoke to Evan, but Lucilla felt slighted.
She walked from the room, wondering why she felt so
drawn to him and so ready to sacrifice her pride and

maybe a great deal more for the sake of a smile from the
surgeon.

When the two men followed her into the theatre some
minutes later, Lucilla was busily checking the supply and
layout of the gleaming instruments on a draped tray, a
deceptively slight figure in the green gown with her
glorious hair bundled out of sight and only the grey eyes
with their sweep of long, thick lashes and delicately
arched brows showing above the surgical mask.

A staff nurse joined her with a pack of sterile drapes
that would be used to cover most of the patient's body
during surgery. 'Evan's going to do a bikini section, isn't
he?' She referred to the kind of surgery that was popular
with mothers who needed or chose to be delivered by
Caesarean because the incision left a scar across the
lower abdomen that could be concealed even when
wearing a bikini.

Lucilla glanced up briefly. 'Yes. Showing off his party
piece for the new SSO's benefit,' she said lightly.

'Oh, I don't think it's that,' Jane defended earnestly,
taking her seriously. 'I believe the patient asked for it.'

'I expect she did.' Evan had won a local reputation as a
gynae and obstetric surgeon for his skill with the knife
and neatness with the needle, and local mothers cla-
moured for his services. Lucilla went on with her task,
mentally revising procedure as her hands dealt deftly
with the familiar tools of the surgeon's trade. She usually
enjoyed working with Evan, but she wondered if it
would be much fun that morning. For the unsmiling Paul
Savidge would be breathing down her neck and watching
every move, she thought wryly.

'Nearly ready for us, Lucilla?' Evan approached the
table, flexing his gloved hands.

'Just about, Mr Pritchard,' she returned briskly,
counting swabs, constrained by the watching eyes and
listening ears of the gown-clad SSO.

'Good. We'll have the patient in, shall we?'

Lucilla nodded to the staff nurse, who hurried away to tell Laurie that the surgeons were ready and waiting for the patient. So that the infant shouldn't come into the world in a stupefied state, anaesthesia was usually kept to the minimum in such cases, and Mrs Wells was brought drowsy but still conscious into the operating theatre.

Gentle hands transferred her from trolley to table and Evan bent over her reassuringly, taking her hand in his own. 'Nothing to worry about now, Mrs Wells. Just relax and leave everything to us, and when you wake up you'll be able to see your baby. He's fine and so are you . . .' He nodded to Laurie, who was sitting at the head of the table, busy with taps and tubing and dials and valves of the complicated equipment involved in his job.

Laurie gently eased the mask in place and began to talk the patient under in quiet tones. As soon as she was deeply asleep, she was placed in position for surgery, covered with sterile drapes and the swollen abdomen painted bright yellow with disinfecting acriflavine solution. Then Evan took the scalpel from Lucilla's outstretched hand and made the first incision.

Handing instruments, listening for the surgeon's instructions, Lucilla was conscious throughout of piercing dark eyes that observed her every move. She was much too experienced to be flustered by the keen scrutiny, but it did make her slightly uncomfortable. She felt he was waiting to pounce on the slightest hesitation or smallest mistake. Knowing he didn't like her, she knew he wouldn't make any allowances for her, and she found herself foolishly working and striving for his approval.

The baby was a boy, a hefty nine-pounder, too sleepy to cry and slightly cyanosed but perfectly formed and apparently healthy. Evan roused him to drowsy protest with a practised slap on the bottom before he briefly held him aloft for general inspection.

'No obvious anxieties with this little lad,' he declared
with satisfaction, handing him to the nurse from the
Baby Unit who had been assigned to take charge of the
newly-born infant.

'I'd better run the rule over him before he leaves the
theatre,' suggested Paul.

Evan nodded. 'Good man! I want to have a good look
round before I sew up . . . swab, please, Lucilla . . .
although I don't expect to find anything but some old
scar tissue and perhaps an adhesion or two. Clamp,
Lucilla. The birth canal is extremely narrow—and
here's the obstruction we saw on the scan! Let's get that
out of the way and send it to the Path Lab to be on the
safe side.' His clever hands were busy as he talked.
'Young Wells would have had a great deal of difficulty
getting into the world on his own and caused his mother
a lot of distress. It's possible we'd have lost them
both . . .'

Behind them, Paul carried out a brief but extensive
examination of Master Wells. Hearing the wail of indignant protest as he checked each tiny limb, the soundness
of heart and lungs and abdomen, the response of
reflexes, Evan and Lucilla exchanged smiling glances.

'He seems to be in excellent condition,' Paul pro-
nounced, and the nurse wrapped him up warmly and
hurried away with the baby boy to the Baby Unit.

Soon Mrs Wells was on her way to the Recovery
Room and Lucilla set about organising the cleaning and
tidying of the theatre as the surgeons began to strip out
of dirty gowns and gloves.

'Well, Paul? Successful teamwork, don't you think?
Lucilla's just as good at her job as I said she was, isn't
she?'

Busy on the other side of the room, Lucilla found
herself waiting for the surgeon's reply, and sensed rather

than saw the shrug of his broad shoulders before he
spoke.

'I don't know how Sister Flint will cope with my style
of operating. I've had complaints about it from the best
of Theatre Sisters, I'm afraid. But she's obviously used
to working with you, Evan. You make a good team,
certainly. I'm impressed.'

Damned with faint praise and put firmly in her place to
boot, thought Lucilla, smarting but pretending for the
sake of her pride that she hadn't heard the dismissive
words. She was dismayed by the man's prejudice, his
scornful dislike and the stiff-necked arrogance that
wouldn't allow him to make fair comment on her ability.
She was hurt too, and wondered why she was so sensitive
to his critical and contemptuous attitude.

She had known at first sight that the arrival of Paul
Savidge was going to create problems of one kind or
another. But she hadn't expected to feel such a strong
and unwelcome tug of attraction for him. Fortunately,
she had too much pride to give way to such foolish
feelings or to let him know they existed. She could be
just as cool and distant and unfriendly if that was the way
he wanted it—and he obviously did!

The long day was nearly at an end when Lucilla
entered her small sitting-room along the corridor and
pulled off her cap, shaking out her curls. The day had
been just as busy as she'd expected it to be, but it hadn't
kept her from thinking and worrying about the new
SSO, she admitted ruefully. He hadn't been under her
feet quite as much as she'd feared, but he had been
around all day, talking to people, watching surgeons at
their work, and probably taking critical note of the way
she ran the unit.

Coming as he did from a famous hospital with its
tradition and legends and splendid reputation for research and progressive surgery, much like her own

training hospital, maybe it was natural that Paul Savidge should be slightly contemptuous of the much newer Camhurst General with its mostly routine admissions —or maybe she was just being over-sensitive.

'*Do* we have a date?' Evan thrust his fair head round the door as he spoke.

Lucilla looked blank. 'What . . . ?'

'A loaf of bread, a flask of wine and me,' he paraphrased lightly, hiding his chagrin that she'd forgotten that earlier half-promise.

'Oh . . . yes, if you like,' said Lucilla, not too warmly, feeling that she's rather go home and relax. A day in Theatres didn't usually leave her so tired and emotionally drained, but it had been a particularly stressful day, thanks to the critical eyes and unsmiling hostility of a newcomer.

'Now that's what I call throwing yourself at a man,' Evan warned in mock-scold, hazel eyes dancing. 'Very dangerous!'

She was instantly contrite. He wasn't the kind to take offence, but she realised that she'd certainly sounded less than enthusiastic.

'Don't mind me,' she said penitently. 'I'm just feeling cross.'

'Not with me, I hope?'

Lucilla smiled at the absurdity of such a suggestion. 'No, of course not. With your disapproving friend, in fact. I seem to have been treading on his toes all day, and it's obvious that he doesn't think much of me,' she added wryly.

'Oh, I'm sure you're mistaken,' he said in swift, surprised reassurance. 'You mustn't mind his manner, you know. He can be offhand, but he doesn't mean anything by it. It isn't a personal thing, Lucilla. How could it be?' His smile was caressing, his tone warmly approving.

'I expect I'm just tired.' She felt it might have been a mistake to admit even to Evan that her feathers had been ruffled by his friend. 'This is my first chance to relax all day.'

'Then you need a night out,' he told her promptly. 'A bottle of wine and a good meal and a chance to talk about something other than shop and you'll feel a great deal better, I promise. I'll go and get out of my greens and meet you by the lift.'

He was gone before Lucilla could say yea or nay, and she resigned herself to spending the evening with him, knowing she ought to be flattered that he wanted her company but doubting that she could ever think of him as anything but a very good friend.

She had dated a number of men throughout the years, her level head and cautious heart keeping her out of trouble and out of love. She had liked some men very well and she had been fond of a few, but she had never been swayed by the passionate avowals of lasting love from men who only really wanted to hustle her into bed.

She had experienced the stir of her senses at times, but she had never known the earth move beneath her feet until that morning when she had looked into a stranger's dark eyes and felt that he had only to stretch out his hand with a welcoming smile and she would melt into his arms without hesitation.

With closed eyes, lying back in an armchair with stockinged feet on a low table as she waited for the relief Theatre Sister to arrive, she daydreamed, fantasising the eager warmth of that sensual mouth, the reassuring strength of his arms and the ardour of an embrace that might melt her instinctive resistance and sweep her over the threshold of loving and giving not only her heart but her body too.

Her lips parted on a soft sigh as she thought of burning, persuasive kisses and thrilling caresses. She

tingled with an almost wicked excitement as she imagined that tall, lean body against her own and she could
almost hear the deep throb of his velvet voice murmur-
ing endearments to enchant and captivate her as he
made tender love to her. . . .

'Sister Flint . . . !'

Startled out of her romantic reverie by the sharply
impatient utterance of her name, caught in most undig-
nified pose without cap or shoes, Lucilla scrambled
hastily to her feet, emotions even more tumbled by the
sight and sound of the surgeon who had set her to foolish
dreaming.

'I thought you'd gone . . .' She tugged at her skirts and
thrust her feet into the discarded theatre slippers, her
face aglow with embarrassment.

Fresh anger stirred as Paul Savidge looked down at
the flushed face and sparkling eyes of a too-pretty girl
with a deceptive air of virginal youth. She was totally
unsuited to work in a hospital that trained young and
impressionable girls to be nurses. She seemed to be
much admired by the juniors, and he deplored the kind
of influence that she must have on them, knowing what
he did about her amoral attitude to life.

She was much too lax as a theatre Sister, flirting with
every man who crossed her path, giggling and gossiping
with junior nurses—and she must be burning the candle
at both ends if she fell asleep whenever she sat down for
a few minutes, he decided grimly, whipping up his
contempt for her as protection from the insidious lure of
her femininity that caused desire to stir against his will.

'I didn't mean to disturb you, Sister.'

You do that without even trying, Lucilla thought wryly,
smoothing a wisp of hair from her eyes. 'What can I do
for you, Mr Savidge?' Her tone was brisk, but a smile
hovered, ready to brighten at the first hint of friendliness
from him.

'Nothing at all. I'm looking for Evan Pritchard—I was told I'd find him here.'

Her smile fled at the brusque tone and its unmistakable implication. 'Then you were misinformed, I'm afraid.'

Paul's glance swept the room rather than meet flirtatious grey eyes in a very pretty face. 'So it seems. Theatre porters are usually very good at knowing everyone's whereabouts too. Just missed him, have I?'

Lucilla bridled at the unmistakable innuendo of tone and glance. Did he think Evan was hiding behind the window curtains or under her chair, for heaven's sake! The man was utterly impossible. Did he really suppose she and Evan would risk their jobs for the sake of some clandestine lovemaking in her sitting-room, as his attitude implied? Or was he merely trying to be offensive?

'Mr Pritchard did look in for a moment, about ten minutes ago,' she informed him coolly. 'He was on his way to change before going home. You'll probably find him in the changing-rooms.' She glowered. 'I'd prefer it if you didn't walk in without knocking,' she swept on as he was about to turn away. 'This is about the only place where I can be sure of some privacy during working hours.'

A dark eyebrow soared towards the cluster of black curls on his brow. Unused to rebuke, Paul didn't care for it—and least of all from a Theatre Sister with an inflated ego and no morals!

'The door was open—not a good idea if you desire privacy, Sister Flint. Anyone might walk in at an inopportune moment.' Mouth tight with temper, he turned on his heel and stalked from the room.

Lucilla was torn between annoyance and regret. It seemed they were destined to cross swords every time they met, she thought wearily. She hadn't meant to speak so sharply, but he'd put her on the defensive.

She was troubled as well as puzzled by his open hostility and obvious dislike. Just as a girl usually knew when a man fancied her, it could be just as clear-cut when another man regarded her with an indifference bordering on contempt.

She didn't want to believe it stemmed from the unfortunate misunderstanding of the morning. It seemed such a petty reason for him to resent and slight her, and she wanted to think well of him.

She knew that she was much too ready to make allowances for him, to like him and to yield to the powerful attraction he had for her. It was something to resist, to fight, to conquer before it could make her miserable.

Wanting a man she had only just met and was never likely to have was a very dangerous fancy!

CHAPTER THREE

'HERE she is . . . my favourite nurse!'

Evan broke off his conversation with his friend to greet Lucilla as she emerged from the changing-room, refreshed by a quick shower and wearing a cool cream dress and high-heeled red shoes that matched her slim leather bag.

Briefly, her step faltered as she saw his companion, the tall surgeon who didn't even glance over his shoulder as Evan spoke. Then, with an unconsciously defiant tilt to her chin, she walked on with a smile for Evan, its warmth deliberately excluding Paul Savidge. He never had even the hint of a smile for her, so why should she waste any on him? she thought rebelliously.

'How nice you look,' Evan approved, the mildness of the compliment belied by the quickened admiration in his eyes.

'Nice of you to say so.' Lucilla slipped a hand into his arm, smiling up at him, pleased that she'd put on a favourite dress that morning. It was a boon that she could wear anything she liked to travel to work, unlike most nurses. It was only a short bus ride to the apartment block where she lived, but sometimes it could be too much of an effort to go home and put on something pretty and come back into town to meet friends after a long day in Theatres.

Paul stabbed an impatient finger at the call button. 'It seems to be impossible to get the lift to stop at this floor!' he snapped, annoyed that Evan and the Theatre Sister were gazing into each other's eyes as if they were besotted by love.

Lucilla Flint might not care about wagging tongues and she no longer had a good name to lose, but Evan Pritchard ought to have more concern for his position as a senior surgeon. Date the girl by all means, but it was a mistake to parade their unmistakable relationship under the roof of the hospital that employed them both! Doctors and nurses were expected to be discreet about the affairs that inevitably sprang up between people who worked in close proximity for long hours and in all kinds of situations.

'It's a bad time,' soothed Evan. 'Change-over for the ward staff. You've put in a long day, Paul.'

He shrugged. 'No longer than anyone else.'

'But we were paid to be here,' Evan pointed out, grinning. 'You're not officially on the payroll until Monday!'

'By which time I expect to be reasonably familiar with the place and the people.'

'Watch out for Sister Theatres if you're planning to be familiar with any of her precious nurses,' warned Evan, hazel eyes twinkling. 'She'll be down on you like a ton of bricks. She may look a sweetie, but she's a tartar when roused. Aren't you, Lucy my love?'

Paul didn't smile.

Nor did Lucilla, thankful for the arrival of the lift. The laughing words implied an intimacy that just didn't exist between herself and Evan, creating an entirely false impression, she thought crossly.

There was just room in the crowded lift for them and Lucilla was sandwiched between the two men, facing Paul Savidge. Pressed close to him, she was much too conscious of him for comfort. Her heart quickened and her stomach churned with a strange excitement and she held herself as tightly as she could to avoid actual physical contact between her breasts and his hard chest. She didn't dare to look up into the inscrutable dark eyes in that handsome, unsmiling face. Instead, she studied his silver-grey tie and silk shirt and the lapels of his well-cut grey suit and hoped he didn't realise she was tingling from head to toe at his nearness.

Paul stared over her bubbly curls at the illumined indicator as the lift slowly descended, hard-eyed and tight of mouth, crushing the stir of male response that she evoked with her nearness. He was conscious of the tantalising perfume of her hair and skin, the quickened rise and fall of her breasts beneath the tautened silk of her dress. She stood much too close to him, and he suspected her of deliberate provocation despite the demure way that she kept her gaze fixed on his shirt front.

Swept from the lift by the surge, Lucilla was promptly claimed by Evan's arm about her slender waist. 'All right? Not too crushed?' He spoke over his shoulder to his friend. 'We're going to the pub over the road for a drink, Paul. Why don't you join us?'

It was well-meaning, but Lucilla's heart sank. It just wasn't safe or sensible for her to be around Paul Savidge any more than she had to be. For, like him or not, he had an alarming impact on her emotions.

'Thanks, but no, thanks, Evan. I've just moved into the new flat and still have some unpacking to do. Another time . . .'

He strode off with only a curt nod for Lucilla, who looked after him with ice in her lovely eyes. No love lost there, Evan decided with relief. Paul had been as noted for his success with women as for his surgical promise in their medical students days, and Evan had his own plans for the pretty Theatre Sister. He drew her hand into the crook of his arm as they strolled towards the gates that guarded the main entrance to the hospital.

'I felt I ought to ask Paul to join us, but I can't say I'm sorry he had other plans,' he told her.

'And I've had more than enough of him for one day!' Lucilla declared with feeling. 'I'm glad to see the back of him, to be honest.'

'That doesn't sound like the girl we all know and love,' remarked Evan in amused surprise. 'You're usually the first to make friends with people.'

'I tried. He didn't want to know.' She shrugged.

Evan ushered her into the bar of the pub that was a popular place for off-duty staff to congregate. 'He's a bit on his dignity, I must admit. Spoiled by success, perhaps. He did remarkably well at Benedict's and I wish I knew why he gave it all up for this place. He isn't saying, but I feel he might have blotted his copybook in some way. I could tell a few tales about his wild youth that you wouldn't believe!' He grinned. 'He'll probably thaw out in a few days. He's really a great fellow, as you'll find when you get to know him.'

Lucilla doubted that the day would ever dawn! Studying Evan as he went to the bar, observing the set of broad shoulders and the shining thatch of fair hair and the clean-cut good looks, she wondered why a vision of a tall, steely-eyed surgeon was suddenly superimposed on his familiar figure and why her heart lurched . . .

They went on to dine at Romany's, a newly-opened restaurant. Lucilla enjoyed the food and the wine and the romantic surroundings, and tried not to wish she was enjoying it all with a very different man. When Evan took her home, she was in high spirits as she fumbled for her key outside her door, smiling at him with infectious gaiety. Encouraged by the warmth of that smile, he reached for her with unmistakable intent, and she raised her face in lighthearted anticipation of a brief and undemanding kiss.

Their lips were on the verge of meeting as the door of the neighbouring flat abruptly opened and Paul Savidge appeared with a box of rubbish discarded in the process of unpacking. He stopped short, an eyebrow shooting skywards.

Lucilla sprang away from Evan as if she'd been scalded—then wondered why she felt guilty. She had the right to kiss any man she pleased on her own doorstep, she thought defiantly, dismayed to discover that in future she would apparently be sharing that doorstep with the new SSO.

She had known that the flat was newly let, but she hadn't expected him to be the tenant. She wasn't pleased. It was bad enough that she would never escape his dangerously disturbing presence in Theatres. She didn't want to live next door to him too!

'So this is the new flat!' exclaimed Evan. 'Next door to Lucilla! That makes it friendlier all round, doesn't it?' He sounded warmly enthusiastic, but privately he wasn't pleased that they would rub shoulders both on and off duty.

'I'm afraid I don't share your enthusiasm for over-lapping professional and personal relationships,' Paul returned smoothly, walking on to the rubbish chute.

The vacant apartment in Ashley House had seemed an ideal choice, comfortably furnished and equipped with every convenience and situated not too far from the hospital. Now he wished he'd made enquiries about his immediate neighbour before signing a three-year lease, to coincide with the term of his contract at the Camhurst General.

Torn between a reluctance to seem pushy and a natural wish to be neighbourly, Lucilla gave way to impulse. Inserting her key in the lock, she said brightly over her shoulder: 'Do shout if there's anything you need. I know what moving in can be like—absolute chaos! It usually takes days to find the essentials and I'll be glad to help.'

'Very good of you, Sister Flint. But I'm reasonably

well organised,' said Paul, so snubbingly that Evan
glanced at him in surprise.

'I wonder why I doubted it,' Lucilla retorted sweetly,
a glow in her pretty face. She turned to Evan. 'You're
coming in for a nightcap, of course.' She spoke more
warmly than was probably wise and bestowed her
loveliest smile on him.

She sailed into her flat, feeling not the slightest in-
clination to extend the invitation to her new neighbour.
One rebuff was more than enough.

Evan paused, feeling his friend had been unnecessarily churlish. 'She was just being friendly, Paul,' he
pointed out in quiet protest.

Paul shrugged. 'Encourage a woman to be a friend
and she'll take over your entire life.'

'I've never had that problem. Maybe you have. But
you've no cause for anxiety on that score where Lucilla's
concerned, believe me. She's a very nice girl, as you'll
find out for yourself if you give her only half a chance.'

'I'll bear it in mind.'

His dismissive tone implied otherwise, and Evan decided to drop the subject. Maybe his friend had good
reason for wanting to keep his pretty neighbour at a safe
distance.

'When's the housewarming?' he asked with a grin. 'I'll
bring a bottle and a couple of girls, and it'll be just like
old times.'

'I don't go in for parties these days, wild or otherwise.
But you're welcome to drop in for a drink any time
you're passing the door.'

'I'll hold you to that . . .' Evan knew that words and
tone and the sardonic gleam in Paul's eyes assumed him
to be a regular visitor to Lucilla's flat. He didn't disil-
lusion his friend. It wouldn't do any harm to let Paul
suppose he'd be poaching on another man's preserves if
he took a fancy to the girl next door.

Following the trail of her delicate perfume, he found Lucilla in the small kitchen, plugging in an electric kettle. She looked up with a smile and then looked beyond him with a slightly wary expression in her grey eyes.

Smiling, he shook his head. 'No, I didn't ask him to join us this time. I had the feeling he wouldn't be welcome. You don't like him at all, do you?' he added curiously.

Lucilla shrugged, feeling that a passionate resentment of Paul Savidge could be as betraying as any declaration of liking. 'Let's just say I'd prefer not to have him for a neighbour. I hoped for someone I could call on in an emergency—if I run out of milk or lose my key or the phone's out of order, for instance,' she added lightly. Laughing, she reached for a jar of coffee from the cupboard above his head.

'You're so sure he wouldn't help out?' Evan wondered if she realised that her thin dress stretched tautly, tantalisingly, over the lovely curve of her breasts and how much she disturbed him.

'I'm sure I'd never ask anything of him! I'm not likely to invite another brush-off!' Leaning across him, she took mugs from a wooden tree. 'Oh, let's not talk about your impossible friend,' she said with a hint of impatience as she set the mugs on a tray. 'There must be more interesting subjects.'

'I agree. As I was saying before we were so rudely interrupted . . .' With a twinkle vying with the warm intent in his hazel eyes, Evan put both arms about her and drew her towards him.

Lucilla put both hands against his chest to keep him at bay. Minutes earlier, she'd been perfectly willing to be kissed. Now, the warmth she had felt towards Evan had been dispelled by the glinting mockery in a pair of dark eyes and a sardonic smile that curved a sensual mouth.

She knew it was foolish to hunger for those eyes to warm with desire and that mouth to take her own in wild, forceful passion, but somehow she felt she couldn't settle for the second best that Evan seemed to represent in that moment.

'This wasn't the kind of conversation I had in mind,' she said firmly.

'Who needs words . . . ?' Linking strong hands in the small of her back, Evan bent his head.

Lucilla supposed she ought to feel *something* as he drew her closer and smiled into her eyes with that warm hint of promise. She didn't—and the unconscious stiffening of her slender body in resistance to the threatened kiss conveyed an unmistakable message to the man who held her in his arms.

Evan brushed her lips very lightly and let her go, smiling as if he wasn't disappointed by her lack of response.

Lucilla was sorry to hurt him, but it seemed best to make it clear from the outset that she didn't welcome his lovemaking. She hoped he would understand the limitations to their friendship. *She* would understand if he chose to end it then and there.

They were sentiments that she found hard to put into words, however. She was a confident and cool-headed Theatre Sister, but she didn't feel so confident or so cool when it came to disappointing someone as nice as Evan —or dealing with someone as dangerous as Paul Savidge threatened to be.

Later, long after Evan had left, Lucilla lay in bed and listened to the music that fiiltered through the thin wall separating the two flats. The strains of a Beethoven symphony weren't loud enough for complaint, merely providing a haunting background for her thoughts. Her mild irritation sprang from the fact that it caused those thoughts to revolve so persistently about her new neighbour.

He seemed to be a bachelor, like many clever and successful men who had never found the time to fall seriously in love. More was the pity, for love could humble the proudest of men, and Lucilla felt it would do an arrogant surgeon a great deal of good to be brought to his knees by one of the women he seemed to despise.

Herself, preferably.

Unfortunately, he was probably the kind of man who broke hearts all over the place without ever losing his own, and she would need to keep a careful eye on the younger and more susceptible of her nurses.

As she drifted into sleep, Lucilla wondered who would keep an eye on *her* and keep her from tumbling into love with a man who threatened mind and heart and body in a way she had never known.

Hearing the rattle of the letterbox, she went to the door and stooped to pick up the handful of letters that lay on the mat.

Glancing through them, she saw they were all for her new neighbour. Mostly bills or official communications, she noticed incuriously. Except for one pale pink envelope, perfumed and hand-addressed and unmistakably from a woman.

Stifling a foolish and quite unnecessary twinge of jealousy, Lucilla carried the letters across the small landing to the neighbouring flat and had her hand up to ring the bell when the door opened abruptly, startling her.

'Oh, there you are! I was just about to put these through your letterbox. The postman dropped them in my door by mistake,' she explained brightly, trying not to stare at the rippling muscles in the tanned torso above a pair of blue jeans. With tousled black curls and dark shadow of beard, Paul Savidge looked as if he'd just got out of bed. He looked more human, more approachable and excitingly attractive.

'And this is yours, I suppose?'

He thrust a postcard into her hand in exchange for the letters. Lucilla recognised the handwriting on the card at a glance. It had been sent by a doctor she had dated regularly in her training days. He was working at a health centre in Cornwall and kept rather half-heartedly in touch with her from time to time.

'Yes, it is. The postman must have been rushed this morning.' She smiled at him, still trying to make friends, still prepared to make allowance for his coldly hostile attitude.

'I hope he won't make a habit of mixing up our mail,' snapped Paul.

Her smile fading, Lucilla looked at him with a blaze of indignation in her grey eyes. Did he really think she wasn't to be trusted with his precious letters, damn him!

'Don't worry, I'll deliver it safely to your door if he does,' she assured him icily. 'Bills *and* love letters!'

Dark brows drew together abruptly. 'Without comment I hope,' he suggested acidly.

'Just the way you want it!' With a shrug of her shoulders, Lucilla turned away, discouraged by the brick wall of his dislike. As she walked towards the open door of her flat, sensing antagonism in the dark eyes that bored into her back, he spoke again.

'I suppose you have a car, Sister?'

She glanced over her shoulder in surprise at the curt question. 'No, I don't drive. Why?'

'Then you travel to work by bus, do you?'

'Usually. Why?'

'I don't know if you've been listening to the local radio, but it's just been announced that the bus drivers have called a lightning strike. No buses.'

Lucilla looked her dismay. The day was long and hard

enough at times without the added problem of getting to and from the hospital.

'Don't look to me to give you a lift, will you?' Paul went on brusquely. 'I'm not . . .'

'I wouldn't dream of imposing on your good nature,' she said tartly, cutting across the words.

He raised an eyebrow. 'Allow me to finish and you'll learn that I won't be giving you the pleasure of my company today.'

The mocking words left Lucilla in no doubt that he knew just how little pleasure she had derived from having him around on the previous day.

'You won't be missed by me!' she snapped, rather unwisely, and shut her front door with a bang.

Paul regarded that closed door with narrowed, thoughtful eyes. Despite all that he knew and felt about Sister Lucilla Flint, he admitted the attractions of her pretty face and the burnished gold of her hair, the trim figure and shapely legs, the sparkling, spirited personality. She was very fanciable, in fact. In different circumstances he might have welcomed the warm friendliness of her golden smile and responded to the dancing invitation in the lovely eyes.

Having met her at last and so unexpectedly, he felt he had a better understanding of the powerful appeal she had possessed for another man. He could almost understand, if never forgive, Greg's readiness to sacrifice job and marriage and everything else for her sake.

Paul didn't understand why they weren't together any more, but it proved that Lucilla Flint was just as fickle and faithless and selfishly heartless as he had always believed her to be. She had taken what she wanted with total disregard for the fact that Greg had a wife to consider—a wife who loved him too much to want to live without him. He might not have merited that kind of loving, but Pam had thought the world of her doctor husband. Even after he had left her for another woman.

At the inquest, Paul had heard the girl's surname for the first time when Pam's suicide note had been read out by the coroner. It had stuck in his memory, along with the description of the girl that a sobbing Pam had supplied when she had turned to him for advice soon after she had seen the attractive redhead getting into Greg's car outside the hospital in London where they both worked.

There was absolutely no doubt in Paul's mind that Lucilla Flint, with her red-gold hair and vivacious good looks and Hartlake training, was the girl who had broken up his cousin's marriage and driven Pam into taking her own life.

How could he feel anything but loathing and contempt for her, or fail to regret that the circumstances of his new job at the Camhurst General had thrust him into close proximity with her?

For his job's sake, he would have to treat her with a modicum of civility when they were both on duty in Theatres. For the sake of the cousin who had been especially dear to him, he must treat her with contempt at all other times—and that meant stifling the stir of unwilling desire for a very attractive girl.

Dismissing her from mind, Paul looked down at the letters he had taken out of Lucilla Flint's hand. Glancing through them, he swore softly as he came to the pale pink envelope with its familiar scrawl.

Some women just never gave up, he thought wearily. Elspeth was being unreasonable, refusing to accept that he didn't want to see her again, making dangerous demands on him. She was threatening to foul up the future just as she'd helped to foul up the past.

Bloody women!

On a surge of irritation, Paul slammed his own door, and the sharp sound reverberated throughout the building.

CHAPTER FOUR

IT WAS A horrible morning, dull and drizzly with a chill in the air. The pavements were still wet from a downpour during the night, and Lucilla picked her way through a succession of large puddles in her sensible black brogues, navy raincoat drawn tightly about her and bright hair tucked beneath the navy outdoor cap.

She had tried in vain to get a taxi. With no buses on the roads due to the strike, taxis were in very short supply. It seemed an equally forlorn hope that one of the passing cars might belong to a colleague who would stop to offer her a lift. Not for the first time, Lucilla wished she could drive and had her own car, like so many of her friends. It was an independence she envied.

But, having lost her parents and small brother in a motorway accident when she was a child, she was overwhelmed with panic whenever she got behind the wheel of a car. Her sister had suffered severe head and back injuries and had been in hospital for some months. By some quirk of fate, Lucilla had survived the crash with only cuts and bruises. She still had nightmares about that terrible and traumatic experience.

She had tried several times to overcome her fear and had eventually given up the idea of a car of her own. Now, with Paul Savidge's caustic words still ringing in her ears, she determined to try again to learn to drive. Just because they were neighbours, she didn't want him to feel obliged to drive her to work on any morning when transport was difficult—or to feel he ought to take her home if he saw her waiting at the bus stop at the end of the day. Lucilla had no wish to be under any kind of obligation to the new SSO!

She had almost reached the massive iron gates of the hospital when a pale blue Lancia passed her at speed, so fast and so close to the kerb to avoid an oncoming lorry with a wide load that its wheels sent a spray of muddy water all over her. Raincoat streaked and legs splashed, Lucilla glared after the car with its distinctive and easily remembered number plate.

She didn't feel that the driver had deliberately driven through that large puddle in order to splash her. He probably hadn't even seen her or anyone else as he sped on his way. But fast driving in such conditions showed a lack of thought for others on road or pavement. Inconsiderate motorists were the cause of too many accidents, and people like herself, nurses and doctors and surgeons, had to deal with the results, she thought crossly.

She dashed a furious hand across the front of her wet coat, and then, as the skies opened on a crack of thunder and heavy rain began to fall, she broke into a run, deciding to sacrifice dignity for the sake of staying as dry as possible.

She reached the hospital with its several heavy plate-glass entrance doors just as Evan strode across from his parked car, bareheaded in the rain. Lucilla waited, holding the door for him, and he smiled at her as he shook raindrops from his thick fair hair.

'Lovely weather for ducks,' he declared with breezy good humour.

'Ducks don't need buses!'

'Buses?' He looked puzzled.

'You haven't heard about the bus strike?'

'No. Is there one? It did occur to me that it was easier than usual to drive through the centre of the town and that there were a surprising number of people walking in this weather, I must admit. *You* haven't walked to work, I hope? Now why didn't you call me?' he said in swift reproach as she nodded. 'I could have picked you up on my way!'

'But it isn't on your way.' Lucilla knew he lived on the other side of Camhurst. 'I'm sure you'd gladly drive right across town to save me a walk in the rain. But it didn't do me any harm, and I don't like to take people for granted, Evan. Not even my friends.'

She smiled up at him as they crossed the wide hall with its appointments and admissions desks, notice boards and rows of benches, passing the shuttered tea bar to join the group of nurses and overalled ancillary staff who were waiting in the lift area. Later in the day, when the hall was swarming with outpatients and people waiting for admission to the wards and anxious relatives, the lifts would be out of bounds to ward and theatre staff.

'You must know I'd do much more than that for you,' Evan said softly, taking her hand in a warm clasp.

Hastily she drew it away, frowning at him for giving the gossips something to talk about, feeling the colour come up in her face as a nurse turned to look at them with obvious curiosity.

'I really must learn to drive, I think,' she declared as they waited for the lift. 'It's such a handicap, having no car.'

'Of course it is,' he agreed. 'I'll give you a few lessons, if you like.'

Lucilla looked doubtful. 'Do you mean that?'

'Why not? My car's an automatic and easy to drive, and I'm a very good instructor,' he assured her, hazel eyes twinkling. 'All my pupils pass their test with flying colours at first attempt. I can teach you the basics and then you can have a course of lessons from a local driving school before taking your test.'

She hesitated, the familiar and deep-rooted anxiety

beginning to stir at the thought of sitting at the wheel of a car and committing herself to responsibility for her own and someone else's safety.

'I might take you up on that,' she compromised, reluctant to refuse such a generous offer and wondering if she might be less nervous with someone as reassuring as Evan at her side. He was kind and understanding, and she knew he had a wealth of patience.

'Any time? How about tomorrow morning for your first lesson? I'll call for you at ten-thirty,' he told her firmly, sweeping her into the arrangement before she could change her mind.

'You're a good friend,' Lucilla said gratefully, bowing to the inevitable.

'I hope so.' His eyes were warm with liking as he smiled down at her. 'I'm surprised Paul didn't bring you in his car this morning, in the circumstances,' he went on with a hint of censure. 'And you wouldn't ask him, I suppose, you proud creature!' He shook his head at her in amused reproach.

Lucilla wasn't going to admit that she'd clashed with the surgeon on that score and wanted to learn to drive as a result.

'No doubt he'd have suggested it if he'd been coming here today,' she said, oddly swift to defend a near-stranger from the slightest breath of criticism even though he had absolutely no claim on her loyalty. 'But he had other plans.'

'For which relief, much thanks?'

She laughed. 'Frankly, yes! He was a thorn in my side all day yesterday!' she admitted. 'But I have to be fair to him, Evan. As the new SSO, he's bound to be concerned about the efficiency of the unit and its staff.'

'I've impressed on him enough times that he doesn't have to worry about *your* efficiency.'

'Once too often, perhaps,' she suggested wryly,

feeling that too many people had been too prompt with the praise of her abilities that Paul Savidge obviously didn't want to hear.

Separated from Evan as the lift arrived at the top floor and Theatres by the sudden flurry of activity, she hurried ahead of him rather than be suspected of lingering too long in his company by her colleagues. She liked him, but she didn't want their friendship turned into a romance by the gossips.

Lucilla had always liked men who were blond and reliable and predictable. Men like Evan Pritchard. So it was odd and rather alarming that she was so drawn to someone like Paul Savidge with his gleaming black curls and glinting eyes and Latin good looks, she mused, hanging up her damp raincoat and changing her shoes for theatre slippers. She was safe enough while he continued to keep her at a cool and unfriendly distance. But if he ever relented and smiled at her with that dangerous charm, held out a friendly hand to her, she might be very tempted to forget everything but the heady excitement he evoked . . .

Walking into the changing-room some minutes later, Julie found her friend clutching a theatre gown to her breast, lost in dreams. She smiled, confident that she knew the reason for that reverie.

'No need to ask if you enjoyed your evening with Evan!' she teased. Lucilla looked at her blankly, and Julie laughed. 'Judging by the stars in your eyes, it was a great success! You were seen together, you know— inevitably! I'm longing to hear what happened.'

'Nothing happened.' Thrusting the foolish and un- likely and too enchanting dream of Paul Savidge from her mind and heart, Lucilla pulled the gown over her head. 'We went for a meal, that's all.'

'I didn't know you were dating him.' The words held a hint of reproach. They had been close friends since

training days and shared a number of secrets throughout
the years. Julie didn't want to be shut out if Lucilla had
fallen in love at last!

'I'm not dating him—not really. We had a drink
together and that led to going on to Romany's for the
evening. It was all spur-of-the-moment, so don't make a
big thing of it,' Lucilla warned, knowing her friend's
matchmaking tendencies and deciding not to mention at
this stage that Evan had offered to teach her to drive.
'He's just a friend, Julie.'

'Just *another* friend, you mean.' Julie was disappointed. Happily married herself, she longed for true
love to come along and capture Lucilla's naturally cautious heart. 'I wish you'd settle for one man instead
of collecting half a dozen that you don't really care
about!'

Lucilla raised an eyebrow. 'Slight exaggeration!' she
protested.

'You know what I mean! You're just drifting,' scolded
Julie, genuinely concerned. 'You need an anchor, Lucy,
someone who really cares about you. I don't know why
you're so reluctant to think about getting married.'

'That's the trouble with newly weds—always trying to
convert their friends to the idea of marriage!' Lucilla
teased. Suddenly she sobered. 'We both know what
havoc can be caused when a girl rushes headlong into
love with a man—and the wrong man at that,' she added
heavily.

Julie bit her lip. She hadn't intended to remind her of
something that must still be painful to recall. 'You can't
go on for ever feeling guilty about what happened in the
past,' she said gently.

'The past has a habit of catching up with the present.'
Lucilla shook off the shadow that threatened to revive
too many memories. 'At the moment, I'm happy as I
am—and much too busy to fall in love with anyone,' she

said firmly, and hoped that was true as she hurried away to begin the day's work.

The first operation on Evan's list that morning was an ovariectomy, and she went along to the assigned operating theatre to check its readiness before she scrubbed to assist him. As she walked in, a silence fell and she sensed a heightening of the atmosphere in the room. The obvious discomfiture of the grouped and idle team of nurses implied that she had been the subject of an interrupted discussion.

'Good morning, girls!' she said brightly.

'Good morning, Sister!'

Lucilla was amused by the slightly conscious tone of that dutiful chorus. Guilty consciences, all of them, she decided. No doubt they'd been avidly talking over her evening with Evan and a possibly overheard arrangement for a driving lesson. Rumours were rife in any hospital, and the juniors loved to invent relationships between surgeon and senior nurse, consultant and Ward Sister, student nurse and houseman. Romance could and did blossom on the wards—and even in busy operating theatres—but not quite as often or with such happy endings as the juniors liked to believe, she thought dryly.

Sometimes it could lead to unforgettable disaster . . .

'Well, it *isn't* a very good morning, is it—weather-wise? But everyone managed to get here on time despite the bus strike—and the rain doesn't seem to have dampened your spirits. I could hear your cheerful voices from the end of the corridor!'

'Were we making too much noise?' a staff nurse ventured ruefully. 'Sorry, Sister.'

'Sorry, Sister,' echoed the rest in chorus.

Lucilla's lips twitched. 'You know I don't object to chatter as long as your hands are as busy as your tongues.' She cast an experienced eye over the room and nodded approval of its pristine state of readiness. Then she crossed to the operating table and the waiting trolley to check the packs of sterile drapes and spare surgical gloves and cotton swabs and sutures that stood ready for use. 'Nothing seems to be forgotten. Well done!'

The glow of her smile allowed everyone to relax. She was well liked and respected, but she insisted on the highest standards of hygiene and efficiency, and heaven help any nurse who fell short of those standards.

'Ready for action, Lucilla?' Gowned and gloved, Evan walked into the theatre on the words and smiled at her before he drew the surgical mask over his nose and mouth.

'Two more minutes . . .' She turned away to count swabs. Usually she enjoyed talking to Evan during the final preparations for surgery, but that morning she was afraid he would inject the hint of growing intimacy into every remark and give the juniors even more cause to speculate on their friendship.

He was used to having his private life talked about by all and sundry, of course. *He* didn't seem to mind what people said about him. But Lucilla knew too well what hurt and harm could be caused by wagging tongues. Hadn't she been forced to leave Hartlake by the gossips?

She didn't want her name coupled with Evan's at the present time for another reason. Maybe it was foolish, but she was particularly anxious that misleading rumours about their relationship shouldn't reach the ears of the new SSO. Paul Savidge was already inclined to disapprove of her and to think her a flirt or worse —and Lucilla had suffered in the past from being tarred with that brush . . .

Evan was in excellent humour, chatting to her and teasing the nurses and swapping items of sports news with Laurie over the recumbent figure of his patient. He didnt seem to notice the occasional whisper or stifled giggle in the background, the exchange of meaningful looks whenever he spoke to Lucilla or sent her a smile, and she wondered if she was too sensitive to the interest that everyone seemed to be taking in their liking for each other.

Later, she was busy in her office with the paperwork that had to be finished before she could go off duty for the weekend. Records needed to be brought up to date, routine operations scheduled for the following week and forms filled for the fresh supply of gowns and gloves and surgical equipment.

Hearing Evan's voice in the corridor, she got up from her desk to switch on the electric kettle, for he usually gravitated to the office for a coffee before going home. She turned with a friendly smile as he paused at the open door.

'See you in the morning, sweetheart,' he said breezily, and was gone with a casual wave of his hand.

Surprised by the abrupt departure, Lucilla wondered if he'd realised the circulating gossip and was doing his belated best to protect them both from more of it. It was much more likely that he was dashing away to get in a relaxing round of golf, she decided. Evan wasn't a vain man, but he would be both puzzled and dismayed to know how strongly she objected to the romantic linking of their two names.

Laurie put his head round the office door as she sat down at her desk and picked up a pen. 'I'm off now, Lucilla. Getting away earlier than expected,' he announced cheerfully.

She looked up with a smile. 'Have a nice weekend —and give my love to Janet.' She knew he was going to London to see his steady girl-friend who had worked at the General until recently. Lucilla had followed their romance as avidly as any junior until the Scots girl had left to work as a physiotherapist at a private clinic in London.

'Will do!' Laurie blew her a lighthearted kiss and vanished. Moments later, he reappeared. 'I intended to let you know that the bus strike is over. The buses should be running again shortly, so you won't have to walk home, after all.'

Lucilla was relieved. It was a fine evening after the rain, but she hadn't looked forward to walking home when she went off duty.

Crossing the forecourt of Ashley House as her bus receded into the distance, she saw a pale blue Lancia parked in a bay, sleek and shining-new and with a personalised number plate that she instantly recognised. She stopped short. It couldn't be coincidence that an expensive car with PS on its plate was newly parked in the grounds at the same time that a man with those initials had become her next-door neighbour.

Lucilla scowled at the car with renewed irritation as she recalled the way it had been driven earlier in the day. Wasn't it just typical of the arrogant Paul Savidge to have so little consideration for anyone in his path? He was a care-for-nobody, she decided scornfully, doing her best to whip up a dislike that might keep her from falling victim to a very different emotion.

The surgeon emerged from the building just as she paused to look at his car. Casually dressed in slacks and roll neck sweater, he strolled towards her, deftly tossing keys into the air and catching them again like a man without a care in the world.

Her heart bumped in her breast at the sight of him, but she turned and walked on with head high, anxious not to appear interested in either the Lancia or its owner.

He passed her with a curt nod.

He might just as well have ignored her altogether, Lucilla thought on a blaze of indignation. She spun on her heel. 'I suppose that belongs to you!' She jerked her head at the pale blue saloon, prompted by a mix of dismay at the wilful behaviour of her heart and a fierce resentment of his offhand attitude.

Paul turned to look at her, an eyebrow lifting in surprise at her tone. 'The Lancia? Yes, it does. I picked her up today.' He ran an admiring hand over the sleek, highly polished bonnet. 'Nice, isn't she?' He was so pleased with the car and its performance that he briefly forgot to be distant.

Lucilla knew little about cars and cared even less at that moment. 'Then it *was* you who drove through the puddles much too fast this morning and swamped every-one you passed!' she accused hotly.

The dark eyebrow rose another notch. 'I wasn't aware . . .'

'Of course you weren't!' Indignation soared at the confirmation that he hadn't even seen her on the pave-ment as he roared past. 'You weren't aware of anything except your lovely new toy and how fast it could go! Just too bad if a few people were drenched by your wretched tidal waves in passing!'

Paul's lips twitched. But he suppressed the involun-tary flicker of amusement along with the stir of reluctant admiration for her prettiness and her spirit as she sparked fury at him, grey eyes blazing.

'I really don't know what you're talking about,' he told her coolly.

'Yes, you do!' flared Lucilla, despising him for the denial. 'I daresay it gave you a great deal of satisfaction to sail past while everyone else plodded along in the rain. No doubt you found it highly amusing to drive through those enormous puddles and splash everyone in sight. Particularly me! Such childish behaviour is just what I'd expect from you!'

Paul inserted the car key in the door lock, tiring of the

angry, senseless tirade. 'Is that what happened to you? Most unfortunate,' he said indifferently.

He took it much too lightly to please the infuriated Lucilla. *'Unfortunate!'* she echoed furiously. 'I was soaked to the skin!'

His smile was scornful as he swung his tall frame into the driving seat. 'Typically feminine exaggeration, I expect,' he drawled.

'I should think the least you could do is to apologise!'

'For what? I'm sorry to disappoint you, but I'm not the villain of the piece.'

Her lip curled. 'Don't take me for a fool! If you don't want to be held responsible for your actions then you shouldn't drive a car with such a distinctive number-plate! I couldn't possibly be mistaken about that number —or the man I saw at the wheel!' she added, with less than perfect truth.

'Nevertheless, you *are* mistaken,' he told her firmly. 'You may be right about the car, but I wasn't driving it at the time you're talking about, Sister. I imagine it was on its way to the garage where I collected it at twelve o'clock. No doubt you were dried out and hard at work long before that hour.'

Deflated, Lucilla stared at him in dismay, feeling foolish. 'Oh . . . !'

'It's always a mistake to leap to conclusions, you know.'

Her face flamed at the patronising tone. 'It seems I owe you an apology,' she said stiffly.

'I won't insist on it. Just be more sure of your facts before you accuse me of anything else,' he suggested smoothly, and turned on the ignition.

Lucilla turned away, shrivelled. She headed for the building and flounced into the foyer, and fumed all the way in the lift to the third floor and her flat. He was a pig—utterly insufferable! Arrogant and unfeeling and as cold as ice! She hated him!

At least, she *ought* to hate him, she amended with reluctant honesty, knowing that his lack of interest was already causing a growing ache in her breast.

The day had begun with one clash of personalities and ended with another. It seemed unlikely that she and Paul Savidge would ever become friends.

Lucilla stifled the wistful thought that friendship had been known to lead to real and lasting love . . .

CHAPTER FIVE

THE NEXT morning, Lucilla was nervously pacing the forecourt of Ashley House some minutes before Evan was due to arrive. Her heart was in her mouth and there was a tight knot of fear in her stomach. She wished she had never agreed to the suggestion of driving lessons, but she told herself sternly that she couldn't go on being a coward for ever.

She saw that the Lancia was missing from the bay where it had stood on the previous evening. She hadn't consciously looked for her new neighbour or listened for sounds of movement or music through the thin walls that morning. Somehow she'd known without really thinking about it that the surgeon was out.

As Evan's car drew up, she hurried to greet him. 'I knew I could rely on you to be punctual,' she said brightly, but she wasn't at all sure she was pleased that he was on time.

'All ready?' Evan's smiling eyes approved her trim figure in the lime-green trousers and shirt.

'As ready as I'll ever be! I'm terribly nervous, Evan,' she admitted.

'You'll be fine,' he promised confidently. 'Get in and I'll explain the mechanics, and then you can take over the wheel. Ten minutes of theory and twenty minutes of practice is about right for the first lesson.'

He remained in the driving seat while he told her the principles of driving an automatic car, and Lucilla listened and did her best to conquer her mounting nerves. There was something about the car's interior with its mix of evocative smells that reminded her vividly of that awful nightmare in her childhood.

At Evan's smiling suggestion, she eventually took his place at the wheel, dry-mouthed. 'I've managed to get as far as this before,' she told him wryly as he got into the passenger seat at her side.

Evan covered the slim hand that rested on the steering wheel and gave it a squeeze. 'There's nothing to worry about. I won't even suggest taking you out on the road until you feel confident about it—and you'll need to get a provisional driving licence, anyway. In the meantime, as this is private land we can toodle about the grounds. There's plenty of room to manoeuvre and few people to get in your way. Just get the feel of the car and enjoy the sensation of being in control . . .'

Obediently, Lucilla put the gear lever into drive and eased her foot off the brake. The car was an automatic and it moved forward instantly. She froze and slammed down her foot. 'I can't!' she wailed. 'I just can't. . . .'

'Yes, you can,' Evan soothed gently. Everyone knew that Lucilla had lost most of her family in a motorway accident, and he sympathised with the thoughts that must be rushing through her mind at that moment. 'It isn't like you to give in so easily. Try again.'

With an effort, she did try again, to please him. She didn't enjoy it, but she *was* in control of the car for a few minutes. Then a pale-blue Lancia turned into the gates of Ashley House.

It seemed to Lucilla that the surgeon's car was heading straight for her at a dangerous speed, and she swerved wildly. Unfortunately, she turned the wheel the wrong way and the approaching driver had to take evasive action to avoid an accident. Again Lucilla slammed on the brake—then she burst into tears.

Evan drew her into his arms, and she sobbed out her alarm and anxiety against his chest while he patted her shoulder and murmured soothing sounds into her ear.

Paul Savidge brought the Lancia to a halt in the allotted parking bay and got out, shooting a malevolent glance at the car which had narrowly missed colliding with his own. He suspected that Lucilla Flint had deliberately swung the wheel at that moment in order to give him a scare, and he was furious. At that distance, he couldn't see that she was sobbing. He only saw that she was in Evan's arms and presumably shaking with laughter at the incident. With a scowl, he turned away and stalked into the building with fury stamped all over his broad back.

'I told you I couldn't do it!' Lucilla said miserably, struggling with her tears, trying to pull herself together.

Evan kissed her, very lightly. 'But you were doing very well, sweetheart. It was just unfortunate that Paul drove in at that particular moment.'

She drew away, bitterly wondering what the surgeon had thought as she slewed Evan's car across his path in that dangerous manner.

'I'll never make a driver. I'm hopeless at the wheel—I just go to pieces! You saw what happened just now, Evan. I'd be a danger to everyone on the roads!'

Evan tried hard, but nothing he said could convince Lucilla that driving lessons were worth the anxiety or the effort.

'I'd rather walk everywhere for the rest of my life than run the risk of killing someone,' she insisted.

'I'm sure there'll always be plenty of men only too willing to chauffeur you wherever you want to go,' he said gallantly. 'Me, for one.'

'It was very good of you to give up your morning, anyway. The least I can do is invite you to lunch.'

'I wish I could take you up on that offer, but I've arranged to have lunch with Mortimer Lloyd. We're playing a round of golf this afternoon.'

Lucilla was surprised. Mortimer Lloyd was a well-known MP who owned a large house set in several acres on the Downs. He also had a very pretty daughter whose outrageous behaviour was frequently headlined in local and national newspapers. Her latest much-publicised exploit had been her affair with a pop idol who was currently awaiting trial for using and importing heroin. It was rumoured that Sally Lloyd had only narrowly escaped being charged with a similar offence.

'I didn't know you mingled with the mighty,' she teased.

'He's a useful contact for a surgeon who might want to supplement his income with a few private patients. He's a director of that private clinic in Cambrook Road. We're vaguely related too—distant cousins.'

'Then you know his daughter, I suppose?'

'Oh, yes. Mortimer worries about her lifestyle and encourages me to take an interest in Sally, because I'm possibly the only person she heeds when it comes to good advice. We've known each other a long time and I imagine Mortimer sees me as a sobering influence,' Evan smiled.

'Very necessary, if all that's said about her is true,' Lucilla said lightly.

'Most of it's much exaggerated. She's really a very sweet girl,' he defended, unaware that he was committing the cardinal sin of praising one woman to another.

Lucilla wasn't jealous, merely surprised that he was prepared to risk his reputation by being seen in the company of Sally Lloyd. She wondered if the MP had him in mind as a suitable husband for his wilful daughter— or if Evan could possibly be angling for a bride with all the right connections despite her unsavoury reputation . . .

She shopped that afternoon and then had a meal and went to a disco with some friends. It was late when she got home. The friend who had brought her back to the

flat went up with her to collect a book that she'd promised to lend him, but he didn't linger. As soon as he had
gone, Lucilla ran a bath.

She was just dipping a toe in the fragrant, steaming
water when the bell rang. Wondering what Graham had
forgotten, she pulled on a robe and sped in bare feet to
the door, throwing it open with a smile on her lips that
faded at sight of the surgeon with his finger poised to ring
again and a sheaf of flowers balanced on his arm.

'I'm sorry to disturb you, Sister,' he said curtly—
having heard a man's voice and the sound of laughter
through the thin walls. The time it had taken the Theatre
Sister to open the door and her scant covering seemed to
him to tell its own story, and he was filled with contempt
at her promiscuity, knowing what it had led to in the
past.

Lucilla felt the dark eyes penetrating her thin robe.
'What can I do for you?' she asked coolly, scarcely
believing that Paul Savidge of all men stood on her
doorstep with his arms full of flowers.

'You had a visitor this afternoon—Philip somebody
or other,' he told her brusquely. 'He seemed to think
you ought to be expecting him and he found it hard to
believe I didn't know where you were or what time you'd
be back.' He thrust the flowers at her with a hint of
impatience. 'He left these for you.'

She clutched the extravagantly large bouquet that was
typically Philip, recalling the postcard she'd put down
somewhere without reading and promptly forgotten. It
must have given her advance warning of his visit, and she
felt dreadful that she had been out when he arrived.

'I imagine you have a lot of callers, Sister,' Paul went
on icily. 'I'd be grateful if you would tell your friends that
I'm not an answering service or a messenger boy. I
obliged on this occasion, but I've no intention of making
a habit of it.'

She recoiled and then rallied, chin lifting on a rush of pride. 'I'm sorry you were put to so much trouble. My neighbours are usually my very good friends too. Dr Howe didn't know you're an exception,' she pointed out, sweetly acid.

He frowned. She was all temptation with her pretty face and tumbled curls and the glimpse of pearly breast beneath the slipping robe. Paul was all man, and desire stirred strongly. Furious with himself for that swift and unwelcome stir of attraction, he lashed out at her with curt words.

'Let's keep it that way, shall we, Sister? You seem to have enough friends to satisfy any woman. There's no need to add my name to the list.'

'I've no intention of trying, believe me!' Hurt and angry, Lucilla shut the door, her cheeks burning at the unmistakable innuendo of the words.

How dared he imply that she had a steady stream of men knocking on her door at all hours! What did he think she was, damn him! He was a brute, deliberately setting out to offend! Must he make life even more difficult for her than it threatened to be with his arrival? she thought bitterly, despising herself for thrilling to the surgeon's dark good looks and exciting sensuality even while he was treating her with that inexplicable contempt.

The flowers were beautiful—and thirsty. With a sigh, she went to put them into water, wondering what had brought Philip to see her out of the blue. Since her training days, they had drifted on a gentle tide of un-demanding friendship, enjoying each other's company when they met, fond of each other without serious attachment.

When he had gone to work in Cornwall, Lucilla had expected it to be the final parting of the ways. But he had kept in touch and earlier that year had spent a few days in Camhurst. They had explored coast and countryside, while Philip bemoaned his broken romance with a Cornish girl and she did her best to give him some good advice about forgetting and finding someone else.

Now she hoped he would telephone so that she could explain and apologise for her absence that afternoon and perhaps arrange another meeting. But she was prompted more by curiosity than the desire to see him again.

For what could have brought Philip to the flat armed with flowers and asking jealous questions of her new neighbour in a way that had apparently given Paul Savidge entirely the wrong idea about their relationship —*and* her lifestyle?

She mentioned the incident to Julie without going into details about the SSO's unpleasantness.

'Perhaps Philip fell in love with you on the rebound and came back to tell you,' Julie suggested with a hopeful twinkle.

'And left the flowers to say it all for him?' laughed Lucilla. 'What a romantic you are!'

'You're too much of a realist,' Julie scolded.

'I expect there's a very prosaic explanation. I just hope he doesn't think that I deliberately went out to avoid seeing him . . .' It seemed to Lucilla that it had been an unkind quirk of fate designed to give Paul Savidge even more cause to think badly of her, in fact.

'He'll phone you, won't he?'

'I hope so.' Lucilla scooped up an armful of gown packs. They were short-staffed that Monday morning and she was helping Julie with a junior's job, unloading a trolley that had come up from Supplies and storing gowns and drapes and packs of gloves and swabs in a cupboard. 'How's the cottage coming along?' She changed the subject.

Julie and her husband had bought a cottage on the

coast at Camsea, a fishing village just along the coast, and were happily spending much time and money on modernising it without spoiling any of its charm and character.

'Keith finished the kitchen units over the weekend.'

'I know it's hard work and a lot of money, but sometimes I'm tempted to invest in something of the kind,' said Lucilla. 'A place of my own . . .'

'But you're comfortable in the flat and the rent is reasonable. The time to buy a house is when you've found someone to share it with you,' Julie pointed out sensibly. 'That shouldn't be too difficult—even for you!'

Lucilla smiled at the teasing. 'Oh, I know I'm hard to please.' She had good reason to avoid any serious commitment, as Julie knew. She had kept every man at a distance ever since she had learned the harm that could be caused in the name of love. Maybe it was foolish, but she was still troubled by guilt . . .

'No one can say you haven't had your chances. More than your fair share, in fact!'

Lucilla shrugged. 'I never seem to fancy the fellows who fancy me—or else it's the other way round,' she returned lightly, and her thoughts flew instantly and unbidden to someone who obviously had no interest in her as a woman. He didn't seem to appreciate her worth as a Theatre Sister, either. He took over officially as SSO that morning and she had a strong suspicion that he would continue to make life difficult for her, on and off duty.

'Are you scrubbing for Paul Savidge today?'

Lucilla wondered if Julie had read her mind. 'Not if you'd like to take my place,' she said promptly.

'I wouldn't mind. What's on his list?'

'Oh, just routine—an appendicectomy, two hernias, removal of a gall-bladder. Nothing that you can't handle standing on your head.'

'Well, that might be one way of impressing our new SSO!' chuckled Julie. 'But it's dull stuff for a surgeon who's supposed to be so brilliant, isn't it?'

Lucilla shrugged. 'He must have known what to expect when he applied for the job. General surgery is seldom exciting,' she said indifferently, as if she wasn't as puzzled as everyone else that Paul Savidge had apparently given up a consultancy for routine surgery in a provincial hospital.

'Telephone, Sister!' A harassed junior hurried along the corridor from the office. 'Sister Morley from NSU —and it's urgent, she says.'

Lucilla hurried away to take the call. She returned within a few minutes. 'That settles it,' she declared. 'I shall be much too busy to scrub for the SSO.'

'Why? What's happened?' Julie demanded from the depths of the stock cupboard.

'NSU have a patient with a tricky brain tumour and Sir Thomas Rudge is coming down by helicopter to do an emergency craniotomy. They hoped to transfer the patient to Hartlake, but he's deteriorating so rapidly that Sir Tom has decided to do it here.'

'And he wants you for his instrument nurse?'

'Heavens, no! He's bringing his own team, thank goodness. But it does mean that I'll have to stand by to meet him when he arrives and make sure that everything's to his liking and remain on hand in the theatre.' Lucilla sighed. 'Why do these things always happen when we're short-staffed and extra busy?'

And when she had particularly wanted everything to run smoothly in order to impress the critical Paul Savidge with the efficiency of the unit, she thought wryly. Something was sure to go wrong; she felt it in her bones.

Later, hurrying from the newly-prepared theatre to her office to deal with some essential paperwork before

the great man arrived, she saw the SSO talking to
Laurie. The anaesthetist had returned from his weekend
in London without the chirpy good humour that everyone associated with him, and Lucilla suspected that
things weren't going well for him. Perhaps he had quarrelled with Janet. Or maybe she had found someone else
since leaving the General. Absence didn't always make
the heart grow fonder, after all . . .

Laurie turned away and walked past her with the
bleakest of smiles. Lucilla looked after him, concerned.
Then she walked on towards the surgeon, who appeared
to be waiting to speak to her.

'Good morning, Mr Savidge.' It wasn't warm; she
hadn't forgiven him for the slur on her respectability.

'I believe I owe you an apology,' he said brusquely. 'I
might have said more than I meant to the other evening,
Sister. I can't now recall what was said, in fact, but you
obviously didn't like it.' For some reason, he had been
troubled by the memory of a stricken look in those lovely
eyes. He had no reason to like or trust her, but he did
wonder if he had been slightly too harsh.

The foolish hope that he was offering an olive branch
died as she met those unsmiling eyes. 'Well, you certainly weren't pleasant—or polite!' she reminded him
with asperity. If he wanted her to melt, then he would
need to make a much warmer apology—and smile while
he was doing it!

'No. I was annoyed.'

'You were forced to be neighbourly and it didn't agree
with you!'

He scowled. 'I didn't take to your friend.'

Lucilla stared. 'Why not? What on earth did he say?'
Philip was the mildest of men and even someone as
touchy as Paul Savidge seemed to be must have found it
hard to dislike him, she felt.

'Very little of importance. It was his bonhomie that I

found objectionable. Dammit, I don't know the man!' he snapped.

She stifled a smile at a mental picture of the extrovert Philip throwing a friendly arm about the dour surgeon's shoulders and greeting him like a long-lost brother. Perhaps it hadn't been quite like that, but it was obvious that Paul had resented a friendliness that assumed a warm welcome and possibly the offer of some hospitality as compensation for a wasted journey.

'Poor Philip! I expect you gave him a very chilly reception,' she said lightly. 'He must have assumed that we were friends, and he always treats my friends as his own. I'm sorry he bothered you, but that was really my fault. I didn't get around to reading his postcard until this morning—I'd tucked it on a shelf and forgotten all about it.'

Paul was startled by an unexpected reaction to that careless indication of indifference. He hadn't known that he was prepared to be jealous of yet another man in Lucilla Flint's life, and he didn't welcome the wanting that threatened to consume him whenever he spent more than a few moments in her company. He hardly knew the girl and he had good reason not to want to know her better, he reminded himself roughly, quelling the feelings that swept through him.

'That explains why he was so puzzled when you weren't there to welcome him. He took it very well, I thought. I'd be furious with any woman who did that to me,' he told her bluntly.

'Of course. You'd leap to the conclusion that it was a deliberate slight, no doubt. Philip always thinks the best of people. You should try it some time!' Lucilla suggested sweetly. Then, seeing the storm-clouds gather in the surgeon's handsome face at the sardonic words, she swept on hastily: 'I suppose you've heard that we're expecting a VIP?'

'Yes—Sir Thomas Rudge. Jesmond just told me that he's flying from Hartlake to operate on a patient.'

'It means I won't be able to scrub for you. But you'll find that Nurse Whitfield is a very capable deputy.'

He nodded. 'I'm sure I won't have any cause for complaint,' he returned indifferently.

That will make a change! The tart words hovered, unspoken. Lucilla glanced at the clock above his head. 'You must excuse me, Mr Savidge—time's running short and I still have a lot to do before Sir Thomas and his team get here . . .'

Leaving him on the brisk words, she wondered if he was relieved that they weren't to spend the better part of the day in close proximity. It was never easy for a surgeon and a scrub nurse who disliked each other to work together for long hours.

For her part, she would enjoy watching a famous neuro-surgeon at work much more than straining every sinew to please a difficult SSO, she decided.

But she almost changed her mind about that when Sir Thomas eventually arrived with his own anaesthetist and assisting surgeon but no instrument nurse.

'Are you saying that *I'm* to scrub for him?' she demanded, appalled, turning quite pale at the prospect.

The NSU surgeon nodded. 'I told him our Theatre Sister is very experienced and can do the job standing on her head—and you *can*, Lucilla,' he told her confidently.

She stifled a nervous giggle as she recalled saying much the same thing about Julie—and her friend's whimsical reply.

'How could you do this to me, Lionel?' she wailed. 'You might have given me some warning, at least!'

'I did mention it to Sister Morley.'

'Well, she didn't breathe a word. In fact, she virtually promised me he'd be bringing his own nurse!'

'He had every intention of doing so, but she's caught a bug of some sort. What are you worrying about, Lucilla? You're no newcomer to neuro-surgery. You've scrubbed for me on numerous occasions,' he reminded her reassuringly.

'It isn't quite the same, is it?' Looking anxious, she reached for a well-thumbed textbook. 'I'd better brush up on procedure while you keep the old boy talking!'

Sir Thomas was affable and charming, and he put Lucilla at her ease within moments. As the first incision was made in the patient's yellow-painted cranium, she forgot to be nervous in the fascination of watching as the surgeon located and excised the offending tumour with the expertise that had made him famous. She forgot to be aware of anyone or anything else as the considerate Sir Thomas led her through each step of surgery so tactfully that even if she had been less experienced she must have acquitted herself reasonably well. Even so, she breathed a sigh of relief as the last suture was tied off and dressings were applied.

Feeling she had played her part as well as possible, she discarded stained gown and gloves and drew down her mask as the patient was taken to Recovery and the surgeons withdrew to discuss prognosis with optimistic satisfaction. Several of the unit staff had managed to find the time to watch the operation, keeping well in the background and maintaining a respectful silence as Sir Thomas worked. Now it seemed that everyone was talking at once, and Lucilla was glad to escape from the theatre.

She didn't expect praise for doing what was, after all, her job. It came from a most unlikely quarter. For, having finished his list in time to catch the last part of the craniotomy performed by a master, Paul Savidge had been reluctantly impressed by Lucilla Flint's coolness and precision under pressure. Priding himself on a sense of fair play, he paused to tell her so when they met in a corridor.

'You did very well at short notice, Sister,' he said, still brusque, still convinced that the smallest sign of anything but professional interest would be too much encouragement for someone who collected men so avidly.

'I didn't know you were in the theatre . . .' Taken by surprise, Lucilla flushed with pleasure that he'd taken the time and the trouble to pay her a compliment.

'For some of the time. A very impressive performance on your part, in the circumstances.'

'Thank you . . .' A smile peeped, for she was ready to make friends with him at a moment's notice. Failing to win even the glimmer of a smile in return, she turned to walk on, discouraged.

'You trained at Hartlake, I believe, Sister?'

Lucilla glanced over her shoulder in surprise at the abrupt question. 'Yes, I did.'

'And knew a doctor called Greg Harman?'

She felt the blood drain from her face. 'Yes, I knew Greg Harman,' she agreed dully. There was no point in denying it. But, seeing the accusation in his eyes, she wondered ruefully how he knew about that friendship and its distressing outcome.

'Just checking that you're the girl I thought you were,' Paul explained harshly, and strode away on the turn of a heel, leaving Lucilla to look after him in dismay.

CHAPTER SIX

'I DON'T know who told him, but Paul Savidge knows about Greg and Pam—and *everything*,' Lucilla insisted wearily. 'I know he does. He disliked me on sight, and now he despises me too.'

With the sun tingling on bare shoulders and already tanned arms and legs, she sat with Julie on the low harbour wall at Camsea, bright yellow skirt that matched her brief sun-top tucked high, feet dipped in the sea. It was glorious weather, and she had gratefully accepted an invitation to spend that Saturday with her friends rather than stay at the flat and run the risk of another off-duty confrontation with the surgeon. She had avoided him as much as possible that week. Now she confided her reasons for doing so to Julie, who knew all about that difficult time at Hartlake, three years before.

'Why should he despise you? You're just being over-sensitive, Lucy love,' Julie declared. 'Even if he does know, why should he blame you, anyway? None of it was your fault.'

'It feels like my fault,' Lucilla said bleakly—and it was true. She had always taken on the burden of responsibility for Cilla's wilful behaviour. Even when they were small girls, she had mutely shared the blame for her twin's frequent naughtiness. They shared everything, didn't they? She was the elder by twenty minutes too. Surely that meant that she must take care of Cilla and keep her out of mischief—or, failing that, stand by her twin and share her punishment? Even when they were grown up and leading their own lives, the belief persisted.

'I've never understood how you feel about your sister,' Julie admitted. 'Perhaps twins *do* feel responsible for each other's mistakes—I don't know. But there really doesn't seem to be a good reason for you to go on feeling guilty because she ran off with another woman's husband.'

Lucilla winced. She had worked with Greg Harman at Hartlake. She had known his pretty but unstable wife with her history of neurosis and depression. She had made the mistake of introducing her twin to Greg, and then had to watch helplessly as they fell headlong in love with such disastrous results.

'You say it the way the world thought it,' she said wryly. 'But it wasn't like that, Julie. Cilla really cared about Greg.'

She had to believe that they'd shared a special kind of loving. Weren't they still together, despite the shock of his wife's suicide? Still happy? Still loving each other on the other side of the world? Deep down, she knew that nothing could excuse or justify her twin's irresponsible love for a married man or Greg's readiness to desert his wife. But it was second nature to stand up for Cilla, no matter what.

'So did his wife,' Julie reminded her dryly. She didn't mean to be cruel, but she had never liked Priscilla Flint. As twins, the two sisters looked uncannily alike, but they were chalk and cheese in temperament. Lucilla was a born nurse. Her sister had drifted into nursing after trying a number of different jobs and becoming bored with them all.

'They weren't happy. Pam was a neurotic, always accusing Greg of affairs with other women.'

'Not without good reason, apparently.'

Lucilla bridled. 'You know that *I* wasn't involved with him—ever!' she said fiercely.

'*I* know it. It's a pity you didn't take pains to ensure

that everyone else knew it too,' Julie scolded. 'Lots of people thought you were the girl who broke up Greg's marriage—and by running away when the scandal blew up you managed to convince half Hartlake that you *were* the guilty party. Sometimes I think you've convinced yourself too!'

'I didn't run away,' Lucilla protested.

Julie looked sceptical. 'Well, I don't know what *you* call giving in your notice in such a hurry and taking an agency job on the other side of London. But *I* call it running away.'

'I couldn't take any more of it. Even those who knew the truth about Cilla and Greg seemed to think I must be tarred with the same brush.' Lucilla sighed. 'I'm sure Paul Savidge thinks so too. Oh, I don't care about that!' she added with less than perfect truth. 'But I don't want it all raked up again. I wish I knew who told him!'

'Evan?'

Lucilla shook her head. 'I don't think he knows anything about it.'

'You don't think it was me, I hope?'

Lucilla squeezed her arm. 'Of course not. Why should you? You've no axe to grind.' She swirled her toes in the sea. 'Anyway, let's not spoil a lovely day by talking any more about it,' she said resolutely. 'It was really nice of you and Keith to invite me over, Julie. Just what I needed!'

'Even if you *were* only asked to help paint the kitchen,' teased Julie.

'That was fun!' Lucilla had enjoyed the morning's efforts and the lunch that followed in the nearby pub that was rumoured to have been the haunt of smugglers at one time. Now she lazed with Julie in the hot sun while Keith worked on the engine of an old boat that he planned to use for fishing trips. 'I envy you two, you know,' she went on wistfully. 'This is an idyllic spot.'

Her gaze took in the picturesque harbour with its fleet of fishing vessels, the knot of local fishermen mending nets and sorting tackle on the quayside and the parade of thinly-clad visitors who strolled in the sunshine or clambered over boats or congregated outside the famous pub to drink its equally famous beer.

Boats bobbed on the incoming tide and the sea steadily crept higher about their legs. The bright yellow of Lucilla's clothes and Julie's scarlet shorts and bra made a distinctive splash of colour against the background of mellow brick and grey slate cottages at the foot of the rambling chalk cliffs.

A launch approached, leaving a swathe of white foam in its wake as it skimmed the surface of the water at speed, cutting its motor on a turn and a swirl of spray. There were two people in full view on board, a man and a girl. He was big and fair and muscular in denim shorts and striped T-shirt, spray-spangled hair glinting in the sun. She was small and blonde, long hair lifting in the breeze that swept across the harbour, wearing a brief black bikini.

'That's Evan!' Julie exclaimed as he leaned over the side of the launch to secure it to a mooring ring.

Lucilla had already recognised him—and his youthful companion. 'He seems to be seeing a lot of Sally Lloyd lately,' she remarked without any trace of jealousy.

'Not the ideal choice of girl-friend for someone with a reputation to consider,' Julie said dryly.

'She isn't a girl-friend, exactly. Evan says she's some kind of cousin.'

A second man emerged from the cabin as she spoke, going to Evan's assistance as the swell of the tide caught the boat and wrenched the mooring rope out of his hands.

Lucilla's heart did an odd hop, skip and jump.

Tall and lean and darkly handsome, even more

attractive than she had imagined when laughter lit up his usually forbidding features, Paul Savidge leaped down to the quay and handed Sally Lloyd from the boat with strong, sure hands.

The girl clung, laughing, pretending to lose her footing on the wet cobbles. Watching, Lucilla saw that the surgeon's hands lingered as he steadied her and that he smiled in obvious appreciation of her provocative looks and figure.

Suddenly, unaccountably, she was filled with resentment of a rival for the surgeon's smiling approval. She looked away, stifling the absurd and unwarranted spasm of jealousy.

'I suppose that boat belongs to her! She's the kind for expensive toys, isn't she?' There was an edge to Julie's tone, for few women liked or approved of Sally Lloyd. 'Just look at her with two men buzzing around! Exactly what she enjoys! She glanced round to find that Keith had stopped work to stare with undisguised admiration at the bikini-clad girl. 'Even my husband can't keep his mind on his boat when she's around!'

Seeing them, Evan beamed and waved and drew his friend's attention to the two girls. 'There's Lucilla and Julie. We'll stop and have a word, shall we?'

Paul frowned. The last person he wanted to see or talk to was the disturbingly attractive Theatre Sister in her bright summer wear, curls glinting in the sun that had lightly browned her body and kissed her pretty face. He despised her, but it seemed that he couldn't help desiring her too. Daily he fought the fascination she wrought, hardening the heart that wanted to melt when he saw the golden smile she bestowed on everyone but himself.

'It seems to be unavoidable,' he said dryly—for although Lucilla was pointedly not looking their way, Julie was welcoming their approach with a smile and a waving hand.

Brushing aside an obvious lack of enthusiasm for the encounter, Evan began to steer Sally along the quay towards the girls. 'Nurses from the General,' he explained. 'Nice girls. You'll like them.' She didn't look convinced; Sally liked very few of her own sex. 'Hi, girls! Getting your share of the sun?' Evan raised a hand in friendly salute to Julie's husband. 'Men must work while women sit and paddle their toes, eh, Keith?'

'We've been working, too!' Julie protested, mock indignant, as Keith grinned and waved an oily rag in cheerful agreement. 'Lucilla had a paintbrush thrust into her hand as soon as she got here this morning. We've earned a rest and a paddle, haven't we, Lucy?'

'Definitely!' She smiled up at Evan, ignoring the chilly SSO. He was ignoring *her*, wasn't he? Yet he'd stooped to speak to Julie, placing a hand briefly on her shoulder in friendly fashion. Again she felt that twinge of hurt dismay.

'Is Evan showing you the sights, Paul?' Julie airily uttered the surgeon's first name. They were all off duty and she didn't believe in standing on ceremony. Besides, unlike Lucilla, she got on well with the new SSO. They had worked together in the theatre for much of the past week.

'Showing him the best pubs,' Evan amended. 'We're just about to sample the beer in the Smugglers' Rest. How about joining us?' He responded to the prompt of a meaningful pressure of his arm and executed hasty introductions. 'Oh, do you know Sally . . . our famous MP's daughter? Lucilla Flint, Julie Whitfield—and the guy in the boat is Julie's husband.'

Keith clambered down, wiping his fingers on a filthy rag. 'I won't shake hands,' he grinned, displaying their condition.

Sally fluttered long lashes at him. 'Nice boat,' she enthused, like a firm believer in the theory that the way to a man's heart is through his hobbies.

'She will be when I've finished putting her to rights.' He gave the hull an affectionate pat. 'We took her over with the cottage and she was in a bad way.'

'So was the cottage,' Julie broke in brightly. 'But we're working on that too—with a little help from our friends. Aren't we, darling?' The smiling words stressed that he was a married man with commitments. She didn't like the way Sally Lloyd smiled at Keith as if he was the only man in the world. It might not mean anything, but most men were easily flattered by beautiful blondes with big blue eyes and brief bikinis.

'Your launch, Evan?' Keith eyed the boat with keen interest.

'No, it's mine,' Sally put in proudly.

'Very nice. Very nice indeed . . .'

She preened as though the compliment had been intended for her rather than for her boat, and Julie's eyes narrowed.

Lucilla looked at the surgeon, who had turned away to study the cliffs with a marked lack of interest in the conversation. He stood with hands thrust into the pockets of slim-fitting cream trousers, shoulders braced in the brown silk shirt and dark hair ruffled by the breeze. She couldn't help admiring his arrogant male beauty and wistfully regretting that they were never likely to be friends after such a stormy start to their relationship.

It was a pity, because she wanted to like Paul Savidge. She wanted him to like her too. Most of all, she wanted him to smile, to speak tenderly to her, to take her into his arms and sweep her over the edge of loving with his kiss . . .

He turned abruptly as if he sensed her wistful gaze, and a betraying warmth stole into Lucilla's cheeks as their eyes met.

Cold, hard eyes looked right through her with that hurtful indifference, then he turned to Evan. 'What about this beer? You've been singing its praises all day. When do I get to try it!' he demanded lightly.

'Right away! Real ale—brewed on the premises! You've never tasted anything like it,' Evan promised. He embraced everyone with the sweep of his smile. 'Drinks all round?' he suggested again.

'Good idea!' Keith seized on the invitation with enthusiasm. Forgetting his grimy hands, he grasped Sally's elbow and began to guide her towards the pub, talking boats.

Julie's mouth tightened. She trusted Keith. Of course she did. It was girls like Sally Lloyd, all thrusting breasts and swinging hips in the too-revealing bikini, that she didn't trust within ten miles of her good-looking husband!

'I won't say no to a shandy,' she declared, getting up from the wall. 'How about you, Lucilla?'

'Just what the doctor ordered!' Smiling, she scrambled to her feet with the aid of Evan's promptly proffered hand and walked barefooted between the two surgeons while Julie hurried ahead of them. She was dwarfed by the distinctive height of both men, one so dark and the other so fair that they made a striking foil for her own warm colouring.

Evan had retained her hand in a warm clasp, and she made no effort to draw it away. Why shouldn't she give him a little encouragement—if only to show Paul Savidge that another man liked and admired her and that she didn't need *his* interest!

'You won't be welcome in the pub wearing a bikini and nothing else, Sally,' Julie warned brightly as she caught up with the couple. 'People are old-fashioned in this part of the world. I'd better lend you a shirt . . .' She darted through the open door of the cottage, leaving them to wait outside the pub. It was unlikely that the easygoing landlord would have raised any objection, in fact. But Julie had no intention of allowing that curvaceous figure to be ogled by every man in the vicinity.

Paul went directly to the bar for drinks.

Evan settled Lucilla in a corner seat at a table. 'I hoped to see you here,' he said warmly. 'I took Paul along to meet Mortimer and found Colway House swarming with party members, thanks to the local elections. Sally wasn't having much fun, so we sneaked away and brought the launch down-river to the coast. This pub seemed the ideal place to stop for a beer—especially when I remembered that you were spending the day with Julie and Keith.'

Lucilla smiled, not really listening to the flattering explanation, her eyes on the man whose long, strong fingers thrummed the counter as he waited for someone to take his order. His arrogance probably expected instant attention in bars and restaurants and shops as well as in the operating theatre, she decided dryly—and was forced to admit that he had a kind of presence that commanded it. Like him or not, Paul Savidge had charisma. It was an overworked word, but she couldn't think of a better one.

'I'd like Sally to know you,' Evan went on unexpectedly. 'She needs someone who'll be a real friend to her . . . an older woman to set her a good example without thrusting good advice down her throat. You're so good with the juniors that I know you can handle Sally. As I said the other day, there's not an ounce of real harm in her. She's just a child playing at being grown-up and making some silly mistakes,' he added with indulgent affection.

Instantly, Lucilla felt about ninety, a staid old maid who'd forgotten what it was to be young and foolish. Men were such idiots, so easily taken in, she thought crossly. There was nothing of the child in the way that Sally Lloyd looked at men with invitation in her blue eyes and age-old allure in every line of her lovely body.

As the girl walked in, the attention of every man was caught by her shining blonde beauty. The borrowed shirt that only just reached her bare thighs was far more provocative than the briefest of bikinis, and Lucilla saw that the man at the bar turned his dark head to welcome her entrance with smiling admiration.

It was probably just as well that he never looked at *her* in just that way or smiled on her with so much captivating charm, Lucilla felt. She could handle the tug of physical attraction, but she doubted that she could bear to know her heart was utterly and irrevocably lost . . .

Sally Lloyd was a constant irritation, with her tinkling laugh and coquettish toss of her blonde head and her flirtatious response to Paul's attentions. To offset it, Lucilla strove to convey an intimacy that didn't exist between herself and Evan.

It didn't matter that others might be misled. It seemed strangely important to convince Paul Savidge that she was indifferent to the charm that could impress silly girls like Sally Lloyd.

Maybe it was foolish to encourage Evan so openly and with no real intention of allowing their friendship to become anything more. But it was even more foolish to hanker for someone who showed his dislike of her so plainly, and there could be nothing but heartache in store for her if she fell in love with him. For the new SSO seemed to have a smile or a friendly word for everyone but herself, and Lucilla didn't doubt that it was a deliberate and slighting exclusion.

He didn't like her, and it seemed he didn't care who knew it . . .

'We're going for a trip round the bay when we've finished our drinks,' Keith announced with satisfaction, having successfully angled an invitation from Sally to try out her launch. 'How about it, girls? Fancy it?'

'Lovely,' Julie enthused, to please him. She didn't want to go, but she had no intention of letting him go without her. 'You'll enjoy that, won't you, Lucy? You love the sea.'

Lucilla looked up from arranging to meet Evan for dinner. 'Sounds fun,' she agreed, smiling.

Paul had overheard Evan's invitation and her prompt acceptance. He might appear to be indulging Sally in laughing flirtation, but in fact he was closely observing his friend's revealing attitude to the Theatre Sister. He was dismayed to discover how much he disliked the implication of their intimacy.

A woman had the right to sleep around if she wished, of course. She shouldn't be surprised if a man despised her for it, he thought grimly. Even when he ached to possess her for himself.

Paul felt the familiar stir of longing for the slender, pretty girl as Lucilla walked along the quay with her friends, a slant of sunshine finding the gold in her hair. Laughing and talking in excited anticipation of the boat trip, she was animated to heart-catching loveliness. She was so vibrant, so alive, so breathtakingly desirable. She was a woman to love . . . if he had never known the truth about her!

Lucilla paused to adjust a sandal strap while the others went on board. She was the last to board the launch, and Paul held out a hand to her in peremptory fashion.

'Watch your step, Sister. The tide's on the turn.'

'I can manage,' she said proudly, ignoring his offer of assistance, smarting at that insistence on crushing formality at such a time.

'Give me your hand!' he commanded brusquely. 'Or you'll find yourself in the water.'

Reluctantly, she gave him her hand and felt his fingers

close over her own in a strong, bruising grip. Flustered by the falter of her heart at his touch, she scrambled over the side of the boat and was thrown off balance as it rocked with the swell. Instantly, Paul caught and steadied her with an arm about her, drawing her close.

The perfume of her hair and skin, the sweet femininity of her, shocked and seared his senses. The blood coursed hotly through him to trigger a desire fiercer and more insistent than anything he had ever known. He wanted her . . . *so much! Too much!* The spell of her enchantment threatened to bind him for ever if he once admitted its power over his mind and heart and body.

'You're right—it isn't as easy as it looks!' Lucilla lifted her face to him with a rueful laugh at her awkwardness and looked deep into eyes that held a burn in their depths to shiver her spine and quicken her to sudden, melting desire.

He held her gaze for a seeming eternity of a second and then released her abruptly, an unmistakable setting aside of unwanted temptation.

'Are you all right?' he demanded, harsh with the need to conceal and conquer that unexpected assault on his emotions.

Lucilla nodded, forcing a smile, too shaken to speak by that timeless moment when she had stood in his arms and drowned in desire. She knew his body had throbbed with instinctive male response. She had seen the naked hunger in those dark eyes and shrunk from it even while her own body was clamouring for him in return.

She hurried past him to a seat in the rear of the launch, desperately wishing that Paul Savidge had never come to Camhurst. At first meeting, she had sensed the high-powered sexuality of the man and its threat to her peace of mind. Now she knew that she was only safe while she clung to a determined dislike of him and steered clear of loving him.

For if liking and loving and longing should ever combine, nothing on earth could keep her out of his dangerous embrace.

CHAPTER SEVEN

HOT and tired, Lucilla shifted her weight from one aching foot to the other. The surgeon glanced up with a frown in the dark eyes above the surgical mask. She kept her gaze on the array of instruments beneath her hovering hand, pretending not to notice the flicker of displeasure. Reflecting the brightness of overhead arc lamps, the instruments swam slightly before eyes that felt gritty from the strain of concentration.

She was working with Paul Savidge for the first time since he had taken over as SSO, and she felt as if every nerve was at full stretch. Julie was off duty and it had fallen to Lucilla to scrub for the pyelithotomy, complicated surgery to remove a stone from the pelvis of the kidney. It seemed that nothing and no one could please the surgeon, least of all herself. He was living up to his name with a vengeance, in savage mood and venting a savage irony on anyone who fell foul of him.

Even the assisting surgeon seemed to be affected by the tension, accidentally nicking an artery. The cavity filled with blood. 'Sorry about that . . .' He hastily applied a clamp that Lucilla promptly passed to him.

Paul glowered. 'If you ever tire of a career in surgery, you'll make a bloody good butcher,' he growled.

Neil Clifton exchanged a wry glance with Lucilla, and her eyes smiled at him in warm sympathy over her mask.

'Swab, Sister! You aren't paying attention!' The impatient surgeon indicated the pool of blood that made it difficult for him to work in the region of the kidney.

'I'm sorry . . .' She mopped up the blood and put the

used swab into a receiver that was whisked away by a hovering nurse.

'Thank you. Now perhaps we can get on . . .' Paul bent over his patient with an air of exasperation.

Lucilla burned with indignation. Unnerved by his scowling mood, she had made some trifling mistakes that further undermined her confidence. She was on the defensive not only because he had turned her emotions upside down and inside out but also because he was openly critical of her work. Heaven knew why she found him so disturbingly attractive, she thought ruefully, watching as the powerful, well-shaped hands probed for the offending stone.

At the patient's head, Laurie kept constant check on respiration and blood pressure and cardiac rhythm as he monitored the level of unconsciousness. Few operations were performed in the tense and breathless hush depicted by film directors. As usual, he talked to the nurses in light, bantering vein as he worked, untroubled by the surgeon's black mood.

Suddenly Paul looked up and snapped: 'You're employed to anaesthetise the patient and not to further your amorous pursuit of the nurses, Jesmond. For God's sake, be quiet!'

Good-natured Laurie grinned and resumed his study of dials and valves. But the remark rankled. No one liked public rebuke, after all. He had every sympathy with Lucilla, who seemed to be bearing the main brunt of the SSO's bad temper.

Something fell with a clatter at the back of the room, and Lucilla turned with a reproving frown in her grey eyes. The offending junior nurse stooped to retrieve the scissors that had slipped from the tray she was taking to the autoclave.

Paul spun, dark eyes glittering and dark brows ominously drawn together. 'Out!' he ordered with a jerk of his dark head. 'And don't come back, Nurse. I don't want to see you in here again this morning!'

It was autocratic, brooking neither hesitation nor argument. The girl threw a startled, enquiring glance at Lucilla.

She nodded. 'I'm sure you can be of more use elsewhere at the moment, Nurse,' she said briskly, thankful that the girl could be spared at that stage of surgery. She knew she ought to protest at the summary dismissal of one of her nurses, but Paul was obviously in no mood to be challenged.

The young nurse scuttled for the door, probably not sorry to escape the uneasy atmosphere of the theatre and the lash of the surgeon's tongue. Lucilla almost wished she could down tools and walk out too. It would show Paul Savidge just what she thought of his arrogant attitude. But Theatre Sisters didn't go on strike in the middle of surgery just because they had to work with bad-tempered surgeons.

As Paul turned back to the table, their eyes met. Indignant grey clashed head-on with exasperated dark blue, and the blaze in those beautiful eyes threatened to melt the ice that he had packed about his heart to protect himself from her insidious appeal. An almost tender amusement struggled with his irritation—and lost.

'Your nurses lack discipline, Sister,' he said brusquely, knowing that the efficiency of the unit was her pride. 'A month at Benedict's would do most of them a great deal of good!'

'Even Benedict's nurses must drop things on occasions,' Lucilla returned pleasantly, knowing he was being deliberately offensive and refusing to be drawn into open argument but unable to stay silent while he criticised her excellent team of nurses. 'I can't accept that you have any cause for complaint.'

'Naturally. Your standards are considerably lower

than mine in a number of ways,' he snapped.

Shocked and hurt by the words that seemed to rake up
the past and lump her with her irresponsible and amoral
twin, Lucilla despaired of his unrelenting attitude. She
didn't understand it. How could it concern him if Cilla
had flouted all the rules to elope with a married surgeon
or if Greg's wife had killed herself as a result? Was he
really so rigid in his disapproval of such behaviour that it
extended even to Cilla's undeserving sister? It seemed
unreasonable and unfair and unnecessarily hurtful.

Seeing the look in her eyes, Laurie felt compelled to
utter a protest. He didn't know what their private quarrel was about, but Savidge had no right to drag it into the
public arena of the operating theatre. The listening
juniors were bug-eyed!

'Fight fair if you must fight, Savidge,' he said lightly,
with a warning glance at the interested team.

The surgeon looked at him coldly. 'I trust your concern for the patient at least equals your concern for
Sister Flint's sensitivity. Otherwise, I'm wasting my
time.'

Laurie half rose, tense and angry, fair face reddening
at the implication that his work could be affected by his
personal feelings. 'I'll take so much, Savidge! But you're
going too far . . .'

'Leave it, Laurie!' Lucilla said sharply, fearing for the
patient's safety if either man lost his temper.

The anaesthetist reluctantly subsided into his seat,
shrugging. But the resentment in his blue eyes told her
that the matter was only left for the moment. Lucilla
wondered wryly if Paul Savidge really wanted to alienate
everyone. He was an enigma, a man of moods.

She reminded herself that brilliant surgeons were
often temperamental, spoiled by the awe and admiration of less clever colleagues and too apt to believe they
were a law unto themselves. At that moment, she felt

that she'd much rather work with anyone but an un-
deniably clever man who thought he could trample on
everyone's feelings and be forgiven because of his skill
and the reputation he had brought with him from
Benedict's.

He wasn't forthcoming about his reasons for leaving
that famous hospital with all its opportunities for an
ambitious surgeon. He had come to Camhurst with a
sizeable chip on his shoulder, it seemed to Lucilla. She
longed to break down the barrier that kept her so firmly
on the other side of friendship. She was sure there was
warmth and humour and kindness and the capacity for
real and lasting love behind the forbidding granite of his
reserve.

Ever since he had come to work at the General, there
had been a slight ache in her breast for something more
to her life than nursing and dating men who didn't mean
very much. Julie was right—she *did* need an anchor.

She needed to love—and be loved.

But the man who could bring about that miracle kept
her firmly at arm's length, as if the bright flame of mutual
passion had never sparked between them in that one
brief moment . . .

'Suture, Sister!'

Lucilla blinked and then slapped the threaded needle-
holder into the surgeon's outstretched hand.

Paul's dark eyes narrowed as he wondered what had
brought that dreamy look into her lovely eyes—and
thought he knew. A spasm of anger shook him.

'If you'd try to keep your mind on what you're supposed to be doing instead of dreaming about one or
other of your boy-friends, I'd appreciate it—and the
patient would certainly benefit!' he snapped.

A nurse drew in her breath on a gasp of surprise at the
unprecedented attack of surgeon on Theatre Sister. Neil
Clifton looked wary. Laurie continued to check the

tubing and adjust the dials of his equipment as if he
wasn't inwardly seething, and determined to take the
man to task on Lucilla's behalf as soon as possible.

Grey eyes sparkling, Lucilla was tempted to fire a
furious retort, but training checked the angry words just
in time. A clash of personalities in the middle of delicate
surgery could be highly dangerous for all concerned, she
reminded herself sensibly.

But he was a pig! Rude and arrogant, setting everyone
on edge with his tongue and his temper. She hoped he
wasn't prone to such moods, or the future looked pretty
bleak for a Theatre Sister who had to work with him
almost every day—particularly if she was foolish enough
to fall in love with him . . .

'Will you be much longer Savidge? Your patient is
showing signs of distress.' Laurie's warning words broke
the tension that seemed to threaten an outbreak of
hostilities between surgeon and Theatre Sister.

'I've almost finished. With a little co-operation, I
should be sewing up very shortly.' On the curt words,
Paul glanced meaningfully at the gowned girl who had
begun to set out the instruments he needed for the final
stage of surgery.

Lucilla's hands trembled slightly, but she was much
too well trained to betray how much she minded the way
he had spoken and what he had said. She had every right
to be angry, he admitted. He was venting a fury with his
own weakness of wanting on everyone that morning
—and most of all on the woman who had triggered the
unwelcome need.

The real danger lay in wanting her with more than
ordinary passion. Women he had known in the past
paled in comparison with the vivid, vibrant Lucilla Flint.
Paul was afraid, deep down, that the girl with the
sunshine smile and independent spirit and fickle nature
might become of real and lasting importance if he

allowed her to steal even a little way into his heart.

He straightened, flexing his hands,

'All right to close, Sister?'

It was routine procedure. Paul waited, briefly closing tired eyes against the glare of harsh lighting while the Theatre Sister checked used instruments and a nurse counted dirty swabs and checked the total with the chalked number on the blackboard. A surgeon had to be sure he hadn't exchanged a kidney stone for something that was potentially more lethal!

'All accounted for, Mr Savidge,' Lucilla assured the surgeon with a decided chill in her tone. She might feel she could forgive him anything, but she didn't intend to betray that foolish weakness.

She watched him suture with rapid thrusts of the needle. Soon he stepped away from the table with sweat glistening on his brow and a deep furrow of concentration etched between his eyes.

'You can finish off here, Clifton. Put in a drainage tube and some securing stitches and then Sister can dress the wound.' He turned to Laurie. 'How is she now?'

'Stable—and her colour's improving. I think she'll do . . .' Laurie used hospital terminology for patients who were expected to make a full recovery from illness or surgery. 'But it took rather longer than I liked.'

'Longer than *I* liked too. Or anticipated,' Paul admitted frankly. 'Sonic dispersal would have been a boon, but I suspect it will be some time before progress catches up with Camhurst. However, old-fashioned methods are still effective, and the lady must be glad to be rid of that stone.' Stripping off his gloves, he dropped them one by one into the receiver held out to him by a nurse. 'I'm grateful to have had a good man at your end, Jesmond,' he added.

The warmth of the unexpected words erased the lingering sting of earlier remarks. Fully aware of the pressures on a surgeon's skill and temper, Laurie smiled, shrugged. 'I do my best to keep the customers alive,' he returned with characteristic flippancy.

Paul looked at him intently, then he nodded, acquitting the man of malice. 'As we all do,' he said brusquely.

Neil Clifton moved out of Lucilla's way so that she could cover the wound with sterile dressings. A nurse scurried for the trolley and theatre porters to take the patient to Recovery. The assisting surgeon turned to the SSO, impressed by his expertise, his admiration overcoming the resentment of earlier criticism.

'That was very well done, sir,' he enthused.

'It was competent,' Paul amended. 'You can do as well—and maybe better, with a little more experience. You have good hands and a sound grasp of technique . . . and possibly more patience than I have,' he added with dry humour that caused a ripple of amusement and an exchange of raised eyebrows among the relaxing theatre staff.

Neil blinked at the praise from a man who had spent much of the day hurling abuse at heads and had effectively made him feel like a blundering idiot instead of a qualified surgeon.

'Good of you to say so, sir,' he said, gratified.

'Your main failing is that you seem to equate speed with efficiency. Wielding a scalpel as though you're about to fight a duel may look good, but it doesn't actually contribute to the patient's chances of survival, you know.' With a slight smile, Paul echoed the caustic comments that a very famous surgeon had once addressed to him in his days as a junior houseman at Benedict's. He had learned economy of movement from that particular master of surgery and he felt it was a good lesson to pass on to an ambitious young registrar.

Neil reddened, admitting the validity of the criticism.

'I'll try to remember,' he grinned.

'You're a very useful assistant. Don't be put off by my manner. As you've discovered, I have a low tolerance threshold and a quick temper. I daresay you'll get used to both.'

The words were meant for all the staff. It was as near as he'd get to an apology. Paul was well aware that he had earned himself a few unprintable names during the long day in the operating theatre.

He moved out of the pool of light that centred on the table and a nurse hurried to untie the strings of his gown. Pulling down his mask, he thanked her with a smile that brought a blush to her cheeks and a slight confusion to her manner.

Busy with the transfer of the patient from table to stretcher trolley, Lucilla nevertheless had time to notice that Paul made a point of saying something warm or kind or approving to everyone but herself.

Her gaze followed him as he went into the scrub annexe, tossing his gown into a dirty bin and exchanging a friendly word with Neil Clifton. She felt snubbed. Maybe she *was* only doing her job, as his attitude implied, but she would have appreciated a word of approval.

Despite one or two fumbles and the moment when she had handed him a large Langenbeck retractor instead of a small one and he had thrown it down with an impatient growl, Lucilla felt she hadn't done too badly. But he hadn't made any allowance for the fact that she wasn't familiar with his style, she thought dispiritedly, feeling she'd failed a test that a very critical surgeon had set for her.

She was struggling with the problems of the duty rota for the nurses when Laurie came into the office. Lucilla looked up, smiling.

'Going home now?' she asked lightly, before she

realised that he was rigid with a rare resentment.

'Before I completely lose my cool and punch Savidge on the nose,' he agreed grimly.

'Oh dear! What now?'

'I had a word with him about the way he spoke to you in theatre, and he was bloody offensive.'

'Oh, Laurie! I wish you hadn't!' Lucilla was touched by his readiness to take up the cudgels in her defence, but she doubted that it had done any good—or endeared her to Paul Savidge.

'Do you think I'd let him talk to you that way in front of the juniors and not say a word in protest? He had no right to make you look small, and I told him just what I thought of his churlish behaviour!'

'I'm sure he was suitably chastened,' Lucilla said dryly.

'No. He said that someone with as much to say for herself as you didn't need a champion and that I should leave you to fight your own battles. Mind my own business, in other words. He said a few more things that I won't repeat. What the devil's eating away at him, Lucy? He went out of his way to be unpleasant to everyone today.'

'I don't know. He isn't likely to confide in me, is he?' Laurie knew about her initial brush with the new SSO and the uneasy truce that had resulted. Sometimes she felt that Paul Savidge had come to Camhurst for the express purpose of turning her whole world topsy-turvy and undoing all her efforts to make the unit a friendly as well as an efficient place to work.

'Too clever for his own good, that's the trouble. The arrogant swine thinks he can say and do what he likes!' Some of the surgeon's remarks still rankled.

'At least he doesn't swear and throw things,' Lucilla said lightly, pouring oil on troubled waters. 'Having worked with that kind, I'm counting my blessings,

Laurie. And he's a marvellous surgeon—that's a compensation.'

Irritation ebbing before the warm sweetness of her smile, Laurie perched on the desk, long legs swinging. He was fond of Lucilla, although it wasn't the romantic interest that Savidge had implied. 'He can't fault *your* work, either. No matter how he tries!'

'I don't know about that! Have you ever seen me quite so clumsy—not to mention that stupid mistake with the retractor!'

'We were all put off by his scowls and growls,' Laurie comforted. 'He was really in a foul mood. Woman trouble, do you think?'

Lucilla shrugged. 'I've no idea. I know nothing about his personal life,' she said shortly. But she recalled a pale pink envelope with its delicate perfume that had certainly been sent to the surgeon by a woman.

'Maybe he was apprehensive because he had to work with you for the first time. After all, you do have a reputation for being the tartar who keeps us all on our toes,' he suggested, tongue in cheek, eyes twinkling.

She didn't smile. 'Some tartar! He thinks I'm ineffectual and easy-going and much too empty-headed to be any good at my job,' she retorted with betraying chagrin.

It was foolish, she knew. But every adverse comment, every critical word, seemed to stick like burrs to her sensitivity.

Laurie hadn't realised that she took the man's attitude so much to heart. 'Never mind, Lucy. I think you're a great Theatre Sister—and a really nice girl,' he comforted, and leaned to cap the compliment with a light-hearted kiss.

Laughing, blushing, Lucilla pushed him away.

Pausing by the open door, Paul Savidge looked at them with a glint in his dark eyes and a lift to a dark brow that made her feel like a flirtatious first-year caught kissing a medical student in the sluice.

The SSO walked on without a word, but the slight curl to his lip spoke volumes, Lucilla felt. She was unreasonably cross with Laurie for having given the surgeon an entirely false impression of their relationship. He must think her man-mad!

'Think he saw?' Laurie was undismayed, smiling.

'Of course he saw! And disapproved!'

He shrugged. 'What's a kiss between friends?'

'It isn't responsible behaviour for a Theatre Sister, for one thing!'

Laurie looked at her searchingly. 'You're in danger of taking Savidge much too seriously, you know.'

'Oh, I don't think that's true,' she said swiftly, alarmed, not wanting him or anyone else to suspect that she was having trouble in holding on to her heart.

'You mustn't become paranoid about him. Why assume that he scowled at you? It was my presence that annoyed him. Maybe my words did some good, after all. He obviously wanted to see you. Perhaps he meant to apologise.'

Lucilla looked sceptical. 'He isn't the kind to apologise to anyone for anything,' she declared, believing it.

'Well, he certainly wasn't pleased to see me. He could be jealous, I suppose,' he suggested with a stir of his mischievous sense of humour. 'Maybe he fancies you?'

Not in the way her foolish heart hoped, Lucilla knew. She had seen burning desire in Paul's gaze, swiftly crushed but certainly *there*, sending shock waves of answering excitement through her entire being. It wasn't enough. Suddenly, inexplicably, the practical girl who did her best to avoid emotional entanglement with any man had turned into an impulsive romantic filled with yearning for nothing less than love . . .

She laughed. 'No such luck!' she exclaimed in the tone

that any junior nurse might use when lightheartedly bemoaning her failure to attract the interest of a senior surgeon who didn't know she existed.

Laurie smiled. 'You could always settle for me,' he said, half in earnest. 'I'm not such a bad catch and I'm footloose and fancy free these days, you know.'

Lucilla *did* know. She felt a rush of sympathy for him, knowing that the light words concealed a heartache and a pride that wouldn't let him run after the girl who had ditched him for another man.

Dear Laurie! He was a good friend, like so many she'd made in the past year. So why did it matter that she was hurt and scorned by a man who had only just come into her life?

What had happened to her pride that she longed so much for one smile, one friendly word, one meaningful touch of the surgeon's hand?

Much more important, what was happening to her heart?

CHAPTER EIGHT

LUCILLA's step slowed almost to a halt as she crossed the main hall of the hospital and saw the SSO standing in front of a notice board—tall, distinguished, darkly handsome and so attractive to her despite everything that her heart stumbled.

She was tempted to speak to him. They would never be friends unless someone made the first move—and if they never became friends, Paul Savidge would never know that she was nothing like her twin in behaviour or outlook or temperament. She was sure he judged her by what he knew or had heard about Cilla and that coloured their relationship, on and off duty. She desperately wanted them to be friends if nothing more . . .

'I thought you'd left ages ago,' she said brightly, pausing at his side. 'You must love the place too much to leave it!'

Paul turned from casual contemplation of the notices to look at the slender girl in the slim tan skirt and pale yellow blouse, bright yellow shoes matching her clutch bag. He felt the tug of an attraction that grew stronger with every day that passed.

'It isn't Benedict's, but it has its good points,' he conceded. A Sister Theatres with a sunny smile that belied the shadow of her heartless past wasn't one of them, he thought grimly. But despising her didn't keep desire from leaping as he looked into the glowing grey eyes that were warm with friendliness.

'It isn't Hartlake either. But I've been very happy here,' Lucilla capped.

'Until I arrived on the scene to cast a damper.

96

Jesmond tells me I owe you an apology, by the way.'

Both heart and hope leaped. Was it an olive branch? Surely there was almost a smile in the dark eyes—and for that she would forgive him anything!

'Don't worry about it,' she said with a swift, golden smile. 'We all have our off days.'

'No hard feelings, I hope?'

'Temperamental surgeons are an occupational hazard,' she told him, twinkling. She could scarcely believe he was actually unbending at last and she didn't want him to stiffen up again!

'So are Theatre Sisters who think they know more than the surgeons,' he drawled.

Lucilla laughed. 'Most of us do!' she retorted provocatively, smiling up at him.

She was enchantingly pretty with that riot of red-gold hair framing her face, small waist and tilting breasts stirring his blood and, most disturbing of all, the lovely smile that might capture his heart for all time if he once forgot that she was a ruthless and calculating schemer who had broken Pam's heart to get what she wanted. And, having got it, apparently changed her mind. What other explanation was there for the complete absence of Greg Harman from the Theatre Sister's life?

'Perhaps you'd like to argue the point over a drink or two?' he suggested on a rare, irresistible impulse.

Surprised and delighted, Lucilla was about to accept when she remembered Philip. Of all times, why had Paul Savidge chosen just that evening to show the first signs of friendliness? she wondered ruefully.

'I wish I had the time, but I have a date,' she said reluctantly. 'I'm meeting Dr Howe for dinner, actually . . .' It was impossible to break her date with Philip, to disappoint him again. But oh, she was tempted!

'Of course. I'd forgotten your busy social life, Sister. Stupid of me to imagine you had a free evening for once.'

Paul strode off on the curt words, furious with himself for obeying the dictates of impulse and leaving himself wide open for rejection.

Lucilla looked after him in dismay. He thought she didn't want him, that it was an excuse! How little he knew! She longed to be loved and cherished and looked after for the whole of her life by the man she believed Paul to be behind that forbidding wall of hostility. She wanted to be the one woman he would want for the rest of his life.

Instead, she feared she only evoked desire, a fierce flame to match her own, a wanting that might sweep her into eager surrender if he ever wrapped his strong arms about her and kissed her. Perhaps it was just as well that she had turned him down. One drink with a sensual, overwhelmingly attractive surgeon might easily have led to the very door of her bedroom. She had little faith in her powers of resistance where he was concerned, she thought ruefully.

'Lucy . . . !'

Turning, Lucilla mustered a warm smile for the man who hurried to greet her with obvious delight. She had looked forward to seeing Philip again, to hearing all his news and spending a pleasant evening in his company. Now, unfairly, she resented the arrangement that had prevented her from accepting Paul's unexpected invitation. With all her heart she hoped he would ask her again.

Philip kissed her, uninhibited by their clinical surroundings and a host of interested eyes, and swept her towards the exit with a proprietorial arm about her waist. Woman-like, Lucilla couldn't resist glancing over her shoulder to gauge another man's reaction to that lover-like reception.

There was no sign of the tall, dark-haired surgeon. He had apparently vanished into thin air, and she almost wondered if she had only imagined that brief encounter and the look in glittering dark eyes that had quickened her to wild, impossible dreaming . . .

Philip had booked a table at Romany's, having heard that it was the best restaurant in the town. 'Nice place,' he approved, looking about him with interest.

'It's terribly expensive,' Lucilla warned.

'I can afford it, you're well worth it and it's a special occasion,' he declared firmly.

Lucilla wondered if he was about to tell her he was going to marry the Cornish girl who had been so much on his mind earlier in the year. She would be delighted for him, if so.

'Are we celebrating something?' she prompted lightly, smiling at him as she sipped the sparkling champagne he had insisted on ordering.

He nodded. 'My new job. I'm off to Canada next week.' He sat back to observe the effect of his news on her expressive face.

'Canada? You aren't serious!' she exclaimed.

Philip flicked the heavy fall of light brown hair from his eyes, grinning. 'I knew you'd be surprised. I'm giving up general practice and going into research, and I've been offered a job at the Mauray Clinic in Montreal.'

Lucilla recognised the name of the clinic that had become world-famous for its revolutionary treatment of cancer. 'That's absolutely marvellous!' she enthused.

'Pretty good,' he agreed with a gleam of smiling satisfaction. He reached for her hand. 'I wanted to see you before I go, Lucilla. It might be a long time before we meet again.'

If ever, she thought, studying his fair, familiar face and feeling a twinge of guilt because there was no instinctive protest of heart or mind at his words. Yet she had always been fond of him, and five years of friendship and shared memories ought to count for something, surely?

'It's a wonderful opportunity for you,' she said warmly.

It was the cue he had obviously been expecting, for he leaned forward eagerly. 'It could be a wonderful opportunity for you too. The Clinic needs nurses with your experience and your brand of caring—*and* your Hartlake training. Do say you'll think about it, at least,' he urged as Lucilla smiled and shook her head as though it was out of the question. 'There isn't anything to keep you here, is there? No one special, I mean.'

She knew exactly what he meant. Then she *did* feel a pang as she realised that there wasn't anyone at all who would try to dissuade her if she opted to work in Canada. She didn't know why she wasn't tempted. She had nothing to keep her in England. No family, no close friends but Julie who was wrapped up in husband, home and the hope of a baby, no one of real importance in her life.

Lucilla had never felt so acutely her deep-down loneliness or the lack of fulfilment in her busy life despite the satisfaction of her job. Had she given too much of herself to nursing and missed out on other things? Love, for instance. Nursing provided plenty of opportunities for meeting men and falling in love. Well, she'd met the men, lots of them, but the falling in love bit had never happened for her, she thought ruefully.

Perhaps because someone like Paul Savidge had never happened to her until now . . .

Philip continued to talk about Canada in the hope of persuading her to join him at the Mauray Clinic. 'You'll love it out there,' he declared as though it was settled. 'A new start for us both, Lucy—and you know I'll look after you, don't you? You mean a lot to me,' he added, his voice softening.

Now that the moment for goodbyes was coming close, he was waxing sentimental about her, Lucilla thought wryly, unmoved by the eager persuasion and promise of the words.

'Write to me—I shall want to know all about the new job. And I'll think about coming to Canada,' she compromised.

She *would* think about it. Her contract was due for renewal and she had already been approached about staying on as Sister Theatres at the General. She had almost agreed. But now, with the advent of Paul Savidge and the way she was beginning to feel about him, it might be wise to leave Camhurst while she still had her heart . . .

It was after midnight when Philip took her home. As usual, Lucilla looked for the pale blue Lancia in the forecourt of Ashley House. There was no sign of the car and she wondered if Paul had found someone else to have a drink with him, to spend the evening with him, possibly even to share the night with him. It was absurd and unreasonable, but she was filled with jealousy at the thought that another woman might bask in his smile and delight in his embrace.

In the foyer, waiting for the lift to descend, Philip put an arm about her. 'It's been a great night—something to remember when I'm miles away from you. I'm going to miss you, Lucy.' Smiling, he dropped a light kiss on her hair.

'I'll miss you too.' On a sudden surge of sentiment, she impulsively put both arms about him, smiling.

Her smile froze along with her heart as she looked over Philip's shoulder. With his usual gift for bad timing, Paul Savidge had chosen just that moment to usher a woman into the building. Lucilla didn't make the mistake this time of reacting in guilty fashion to an unmistakable gleam of disapproval in the surgeon's glance.

Defiant, she remained standing within the circle of Philip's embracing arm as the couple approached.

Paul's dark good looks were the perfect foil for his companion's rich titian hair and glowing beauty. Tall and slender in clinging white silk, emeralds at ears and throat, shining hair swept back from a lovely oval face, she was the kind of woman that any man would admire and desire, Lucilla admitted with a pang.

She was very sure of herself. Sure of *him* too. It showed in the way her hand rested on Paul's arm, the way she looked at him with the smiling confidence that implied shared delights and mutual pleasures, long and intimate understanding.

The surgeon nodded to Lucilla, curt and unsmiling, a hint of scorn in his dark eyes. Her heart sank. She was innocent of anything but a friendly and lighthearted relationship with Evan, with Laurie, with Philip, but he was heartbreakingly ready to condemn her as a flirt and a wanton, she thought despairingly.

Philip held out an eager hand. 'Savidge, isn't it? I wonder if you recall—Philip Howe? The flowers for Lucilla . . . ?'

Paul shook hands without enthusiasm. 'How are you?'

It was so bland, so indifferent, that Lucilla winced. But Philip didn't seem to notice the offhand manner that anyone else would have recognised as a snub. Frowning, she walked into the lift. Hurt and jealous, she had no desire to linger in pointless conversation with Paul Savidge and his complacently smiling girl-friend.

Philip ushered the couple into the lift ahead of him.

'We've just been celebrating my imminent flight to Montreal,' he announced. 'I think I told you I'm going to work at the Mauray Clinic, didn't I, Savidge?'

'It was mentioned,' Paul said dryly.

His sardonic tone convinced Lucilla that the garrulous Philip had mentioned it at length. He was the kind who told his life history to strangers at the drop of a hat. It was one of his less endearing traits and exposed him to rebuff from people like Paul Savidge, she thought crossly.

'I owe you a favour,' Philip went on warmly. 'I felt such a fool standing at Lucilla's door the other day with an armful of flowers. It was very decent of you to come to the rescue.'

Lucilla studied the floor indicator, silent, her face expressionless, feeling Philip was making far too much of a trivial incident.

'Not at all,' the surgeon returned indifferently. He turned to the woman at his side, whose tentative smile held a natural curiosity about the exchange. 'Sister Flint and I are neighbours. She has the next flat to mine.'

She smiled, but her eyes were cool and considering as she regarded Lucilla. 'I expect you work at the General too. Where did you train?'

'Hartlake.' Lucilla didn't like the woman or her patronising attitude. She was almost brusque in reply, which wasn't at all like her, and she saw surprise in Philip's quick glance.

'Oh, yes. Paul and I knew each other when he worked at Benedict's . . .' Her hand clutched his arm with a proprietorial confidence and she smiled up at him warmly as she spoke.

Observing her rings, wide gold band and emerald solitaire, Lucilla couldn't help wondering if an indiscreet affair with a married woman had led to the surgeon's resignation from that very famous hospital. Had an ambitious man fallen in love and then been compelled to choose between his career and a woman? If so, the woman had apparently won, which must mean that there could be no hope of happiness for anyone else who was fool enough to fall in love with Paul Savidge.

For some inexplicable reason, her heart sank . . .

Searching for her door-key as she stepped out of the lift, she was horrified to hear Philip urging the surgeon and his companion to join them for a nightcap, ever ready to play the host.

She swung. 'It's late, Philip. Some of us have to work tomorrow,' she reminded him as lightly as she could.

Paul hadn't needed to see the look on her face to know how she had reacted to her friend's suggestion. 'We won't intrude,' he said smoothly.

'One drink,' Philip insisted hospitably, blind and deaf to atmosphere. 'To wish me luck! You won't be intruding, Savidge. I've known Lucy since her first-year days at Hartlake. But I think I told you that, didn't I?'

He said it with an air that instantly made Lucilla wonder just how much he had told Paul Savidge about her in the course of casual conversation!

About to refuse again, more firmly, Paul abruptly changed his mind. The Theatre Sister was so obviously opposed to the idea that he was perversely inclined to support it. 'Very well. But only one drink, Howe. I have to drive Mrs Marshall to her hotel . . .'

When? As dawn broke over the Downs? Heart stabbed by an absurd jealousy of their unmistakable relationship, Lucilla led the way into her flat, left with no choice but to entertain them for a short time.

Philip immediately made his way across her sitting-room to dispense drinks with an air of being totally at home that she hoped Paul didn't notice and misinterpret. Having set foot in her flat for the first time, the surgeon seemed to be making a comprehensive survey of her pictures and books and ornaments as though they held some clue to her character.

She turned to his beautiful woman friend and indicated a chair. 'Do sit down, Mrs Marshall.'

'Thank you . . . but do call me Elspeth, won't you?' Her smile was frosty as she sank into the armchair,

for this was not the way she had expected to round off
the evening—drinks and polite conversation with total
strangers. She was far from pleased that Paul's neighbour was not only young and pretty but also worked at
the General. A surgeon and a nurse who were constantly
thrown together could end up taking more than a professional interest in each other. She made a vain search
of her handbag and then looked round. 'Paul darling, I
seem to have left my cigarettes in the car. Be an angel
and get them for me.'

As Paul went to do the woman's bidding, Lucilla
settled herself on the sofa cushions. 'You say you knew
Paul when he worked at Benedict's? Are you a nurse?
she asked.

'Not now. I trained at Benedict's but left nursing when
I married.' Elspeth flashed an automatically charming
smile at Philip as he put a drink on a low table close to her
hand. 'I'm seriously thinking of going back to it, however. In fact, I've been talking to Paul about my chances
of a job at the General.'

Surprised that such an elegant creature wanted to
return to the hard world of nursing, Lucilla wondered if
Paul was encouraging her in the idea and just how
involved he was with this woman whose plans for the
future didn't seem to include her absent husband.

'We're cutting down on staff at the moment, I'm
afraid,' she said without any trace of regret. 'Govern-
ment cut-backs . . .'

Elspeth nodded. 'It's the same at most hospitals, of
course. But you're talking about non-essential staff,
surely. I gather that your Sister Theatres may be leaving shortly. I was a Theatre Sister at Benedict's and
that ought to qualify me for the job, don't you think?
And I'm sure Paul could always pull a few strings if
necessary,' she added with a confident smile.

Lucilla stiffened at the words. Paul must know her

contract was coming up for renewal. While he might not want her to stay on at the General, it was really too bad of him to be virtually promising her job to his girl-friend! Had he set out from the start to be horrid to her in the hope that she would decide to leave and thus pave the way for Elspeth Marshall to step into her shoes?

Over my dead body! she vowed fiercely. He wasn't going to drive her away from Camhurst with his coldly contemptuous attitude—*or* with his dangerous assault on her heart!

'Paul's got it wrong,' she said coolly, deliberately using his name as though they were on intimate terms. 'I happen to know that our present Sister Theatres has no intention of giving up her job.'

Puzzled, Philip came to perch on the arm of the sofa at her side. 'I thought *you* were Sister Theatres at the General, Lucy.'

She sent him a sunny smile. 'So I am. That's how I can be so sure.' She was sorry to disappoint his dream of having her join him in Montreal, but she was sure he would soon forget all about it in the excitement of his new job.

Elspeth shrugged. 'Maybe I misunderstood the situation. But I've really set my heart on working with Paul again, so if you should change your mind . . . ?' Lucilla remained stubbornly silent during the brief, pregnant pause. 'Oh, well, Paul will let me know if you do or if something else comes along,' Elspeth went on lightly, eyes narrowing at the girl's transparent hostility.

She had no difficulty in guessing at its cause. Paul was too attractive for his own good, she thought dryly, wondering if he had misled the girl with his easy charm or if she had merely fallen a victim to his dark good looks and compelling personality.

'I'm sure he'll do his best for you,' Lucilla said shortly just as the surgeon returned.

'Oh, of course he will. I can always rely on Paul—he's a very good friend. Aren't you, darling?'

Words and tone and intimate smile hinted that there was much more to their relationship than mere friendship. Paul frowned.

'To you *and* Guy. For a good many years,' he countered smoothly, disliking the caressing tone and misleading endearment and the warmth of Elspeth's manner that laid such blatant claim to him. He resented the unmistakable '*hands off—he's mine*' warning to another woman and marvelled that Elspeth should suppose the stony-faced Theatre Sister was setting her cap at *him*! The situation was so obviously not to her liking that he suspected she'd have been happily lying in Howe's arms by now if that young man hadn't issued that impulsive invitation. 'Did Elspeth tell you she's married to Guy Marshall, the heart and lung transplant specialist? We worked together in the days before he became so well known.'

The deliberate mention of her husband brought an angry sparkle to Elspeth's beautiful eyes. 'Paul was best man at the wedding,' she capped brightly. 'Best man in every way, as things turned out. If I'd only known it at the time, it would have saved all the trouble and tiresomeness of the divorce.'

Paul's dark brows snapped together.

It was the first he'd heard of a divorce, although he knew that Guy and Elspeth had been going through a bad patch in their marriage long before he had foolishly given her cause to hanker for her freedom.

He wasn't proud of the affair that had begun as a mild flirtation and snowballed. Cheating on a friend had hurt his conscience and reminded him too vividly of the terrible consequences that had followed when his cousin's marriage was destroyed by a similar affair between two people who took what they wanted regardless of the damage they might do to a sensitive girl.

Leaving Benedict's and London and Elspeth behind him, Paul hadn't expected or wanted her to track him to Camhurst, writing, phoning and finally arriving at his flat that evening with the announcement that Guy was in Amsterdam for a medical conference and she'd decided to look him up for old times' sake.

At least she had had the discretion to book herself into a hotel—and if she hadn't left her expensive furs in his flat when he reluctantly took her to a restaurant on the outskirts of the town for dinner, they would have been on their way back to the Regency at this hour and wouldn't have run into Lucilla Flint and her effusive boy-friend.

Now he wondered if Elspeth had left Guy at last, expecting him to rally to her support and hoping to use him to secure her release from a disappointing marriage. She might even cherish the hope of marrying him eventually.

Well, she wouldn't succeed on either score, Paul told himself grimly, lowering himself to a seat on the sofa beside the silent Theatre Sister. His plans for the future didn't include Elspeth.

They might have revolved around the enchantingly pretty Lucilla Flint if he had never known about her involvement with Greg Harman and its disastrous effect on Pam. But that involvement had been brought to mind with a jolt by the discovery of a framed photograph on a shelf of the wall unit where Lucilla kept her books and ornaments and other personal treasures.

Paul wondered why she retained that photograph of herself and Greg, arms entwined and eyes shining with the love that had discounted everyone and everything else, when the man had apparently gone out of her life.

It was odd how women clung to reminders of their lost loves.

CHAPTER NINE

ELSPETH MARSHALL'S light but deliberately chosen words seemed to strike like hammer-blows at Lucilla's heart, crushing the lingering and very foolish hope that one day she might be more than just an efficient Theatre Sister to a very attractive surgeon.

In that moment, she realised just how much he was already beginning to mean to her—and that was another blow!

The slightly uncomfortable silence kept Elspeth's words suspended in mid-air for a few seconds. Then it was broken by the well-meaning Philip, who seized on the earlier mention of a much respected name.

'The Mauray Clinic has its own programme of heart-lung transplants, of course. I expect you know their unit is named after your husband, Mrs Marshall? I believe he goes over there occasionally to operate and to lecture at the clinic. Does he have any plans to visit Montreal in the near future? I'd very much like to meet him.'

'I've no idea.' The woman's shrug was expressive of her indifference. 'He's in Amsterdam at the moment.' She turned to Lucilla. 'Never marry a doctor, my dear. Their patients see far more of them than their wives ever do—and pretty nurses are a constant temptation.'

'Lucilla has first-hand knowledge of the distress it can cause a doctor's wife when her husband takes more than a professional interest in a nurse he meets through his work,' Paul said harshly.

The lash of his tone cut across the pleasure that Lucilla had felt at hearing her name on his lips at last. She looked at him quickly, colouring as she flooded with

familiar guilt for what had happened three years before,
although she couldn't have foreseen the outcome of
innocently introducing her twin to Greg Harman. Again
she realised that the General's new SSO knew all about
that sad time and the part she had played in it.

Meeting cold accusation in his gaze, she hastily looked
away again, and her glance fell on the framed photograph of Cilla and Greg, taken in Australia where they
had settled, far from Hartlake and all the reminders of
his first marriage.

As he observed that glance, seeing the flicker of
sentiment that crossed her pretty, expressive face, Paul's
mouth tightened in a grim, unforgiving line.

'Referring to the Harman affair?' Philip rushed in,
assuming that Lucilla had confided her lingering unhappiness about Pam Harman's death to the surgeon.
'Lucy blames herself, but it was just one of those unfortunate things, as I keep telling her. Greg's marriage was
a failure and his wife had a history of depression. It was a
sad business, best forgotten. Fretting about the past
doesn't do any good. Nor does talking about it, if you
don't mind my saying so, Savidge.' Philip was concerned
for Lucilla's obvious distress as she looked at the photograph of her sister, far off in another country with the
man whose wife had died because they loved each other.

'I haven't the slightest wish to talk about it,' Paul said
brusquely. 'It wasn't my intention to name names or
drag up guilty secrets.'

The colour deepened in Lucilla's cheeks and his eyes
darkened to sombre hue as he sat at her side, swirling the
amber liquid in his glass, while Philip turned to the
puzzled Elspeth Marshall and resumed his monologue
on the Mauray Clinic.

Lucilla stole a glance at the brooding surgeon beside
her on the sofa, wondering at his knowledge of and
interest in a long-ago love affair with a most unhappy

ending. Had he known Pam Harman? Loved her himself, perhaps? Well, now he was in love with someone else, she thought with a pang.

Paul's shoulder briefly brushed her bare arm as he leaned to place his untouched glass of whisky on the table. The physical contact caused a tingling awareness of him in every vein. With all her senses on the quiver and her heart throbbing, Lucilla was filled with longing for this man who apparently belonged to another woman.

Medical men had to be so careful to avoid any hint of scandal, and it seemed that the surgeon had the shadow of divorce proceedings hanging over him. No wonder he was so dour, so difficult, so unapproachable. No wonder he was short-tempered, snapping at everyone and venting his frustrations on her in particular . . .

'. . . I've been trying to talk Lucilla into joining me in Canada.'

Lucilla tuned in to the conversation to hear the misleadingly possessive words, and frowned. 'You know I can't be talked into things, Philip,' she said with an edge to her voice. 'I like to make up my own mind in my own time.'

'And once made up, you won't change it come hell or high water. Stubborn as a mule!' The affectionate tone took the sting from the words. He grinned at Paul. 'You'll find that out for yourself soon if you haven't already, Savidge.'

'Those who won't bend must break in the end,' drawled Paul. 'Or so my old nanny always used to warn me.'

Lucilla looked at him in swift suspicion of the mocking words.

'You must have been a very obstinate little boy,' she said lightly, but it was an unmistakable challenge.

'Oh, yes. Proud—and I'd never admit to being in the

wrong about anything. Much like yourself, I imagine. Growing up doesn't alter the basic faults of character, does it?'

It was so pointed that her grey eyes blazed with sudden indignation. Realising that he meant to be offensive she swept her chin up on a surge of her own pride.

'Some of us learn in the process how to get on with people and to accept that we can't have our own way all the time, however,' she said tartly.

'Some of us never accept that there *is* any way but our own.'

'Some of us are just born arrogant,' she said sweetly.

The surgeon smiled. 'I should never have said humility was *your* strong point, Sister.'

Puzzled by the cut and thrust of the verbal duel, Philip hastened to pour oil on apparently troubled waters. 'Let me get you another drink, Mrs Marshall... Lucy? How about you, Savidge?'

'No thanks. It's getting late and I must get Mrs Marshall back to her hotel.'

Philip turned eagerly to Elspeth. 'Is it the Regency, by any chance?'

She looked surprised. 'Why, yes!'

'Of course! That's where I saw you,' he exclaimed, beaming. 'We booked in about the same time this afternoon. I'm staying at the Regency, too... only overnight as I've an early appointment in London tomorrow. But it means I can drive you back to the hotel... if you've no objection, of course, Savidge?'

'That's very good of you,' Paul said promptly, giving Elspeth no opportunity to turn down the suggestion, relieved by such a simple solution to the problem of the final parting.

'Not at all! I like to return a favour when I can.' Philip smiled at the smouldering woman. 'Whenever you're ready, Mrs Marshall...?'

'Now, I think,' she said coldly, making no effort to
hide her annoyance. 'Get my furs, Paul . . .'

She was fuming. He had wriggled out of promises
made in the first flush of his passion for her and now he
had seized on a way to end the evening without having to
spell out that he had no desire to end it in her arms, she
thought furiously. She had wasted time and effort in
pursuing him to Camhurst, swallowing her pride, and
she wouldn't easily forgive him for making it so obvious
that he no longer wanted her.

That exchange with the Theatre Sister had sounded
like the continuation of a private quarrel to her ears, and
she wondered just how well Paul knew the girl and if she
was the magnet that had drawn him to Camhurst. Whatever reason he had for leaving Benedict's and London
so suddenly, it was painfully obvious that he had lost
all interest in her. Well, it wouldn't be the first time
she'd welcomed Guy back into her arms as if he had
walked out on her instead of the other way round—and
she should be back in London in time to destroy the
note she'd left for him before he got back from
Amsterdam . . .

Lucilla felt a surge of regret as the lift doors closed on
her last sight of Philip. She hadn't said a proper goodbye
to him, and she might never see him again. Everything
had happened too quickly. In fact, it seemed to her that
Paul had hustled the couple from her flat with unseemly
haste.

Tears brimmed and she sighed. Not because Philip
had gone out of her life but because Paul Savidge
had walked into it, to set heart and mind and body in
turmoil.

Turning away from the lift, Paul saw tears sparkling in
her eyes and felt the wrench of jealous anger. The raging
tensions of the day had built up in him to a volcanic fury
that threatened to erupt in passionate resentment of the

insistent, insidious ache of more than physical desire for a heartless slut.

He put a hand to the tear that trembled like fluid crystal on her cheek and brushed it away, none too gently.

'Tears?' he mocked savagely. 'Cry over them all, do you? Crocodile tears, no doubt—like the ones you probably shed when Pam Harman killed herself!'

Lucilla was shocked by the brutal tone. 'Did you *know* Pam?' she asked impulsively, puzzled by the intensity of that fierce, freezing contempt.

'Very well. She was my cousin.'

'Oh . . . I'm sorry!' What else could she say? she wondered miserably. Having learned the reason for his forbidding and hostile reserve and dislike didn't make it any easier to bear. 'It was a dreadful time. I felt it as much as anyone,' she said defensively.

'I doubt it,' Paul returned cruelly. He looked at her coldly. 'Where's Harman these days?'

'In Australia . . .' She wondered if he knew that Greg had married her twin within weeks of his wife's death.

He nodded. 'That doesn't surprise me. He knew that if I ever got my hands on him he'd suffer for what he did to Pam,' he said grimly.

The venom was unmistakable, frightening. 'It's a lot of hate. You must have been very fond of your cousin,' Lucilla said quietly. A shadow crossed her face. 'I think you hate me for my part in it too.'

Paul had known she was even more to blame than Pam's gutless husband, but he was still shattered by the confirmation of those words.

It had been easy to despise a girl he had never met. In the short time he had known Lucilla Flint, despite the inbuilt prejudice and a determination to dislike her, he had found it increasingly difficult to relate her warm and obviously caring nature to the part she had played in

Pam's tragic death. How had such a genuinely nice girl ever allowed herself to be drawn into a sordid affair with a married man? How had she been a willing partner in an elopement that drove an unstable, unhappy girl to kill herself?

Paul had been almost ready to believe some mistake had been made, that another Hartlake nurse had been involved with Greg, despite the inescapable fact that she bore the same name. A growing admiration for the Theatre Sister had prompted him to want to think well of her, he admitted. Now her words confirmed everything he had ever thought and felt and known about her and made it impossible for him to entertain the feelings that had been leading him into loving.

But, standing with her in the impersonal square of hallway that separated their two flats, he was almost overwhelmed with the longing to have her in his arms, close to his heart.

Despite everything . . .

'You can't expect me to like or respect you,' he told her bluntly. 'That doesn't mean I can't react like any other man to your considerable attractions.'

Instinct sounded an alarm in Lucilla's breast as she saw the twin candles of a very dangerous flame in his dark eyes.

'I'm not sure that's a compliment,' she said stiffly, taking a slight, backward step.

'You don't deny that there are a lot of men in your life, surely, Sister?'

Her chin shot up at the unmistakable implication of that mocking taunt. 'I have several good friends who happen to be men, if that's what you mean.'

'*Friends* . . .' Paul echoed her harshly, his lip curling. Then he shrugged. 'It's as good a word as any, I suppose.'

Lucilla brushed past him to the door of her flat, hurt

and angry. 'I suggest you say good night before you say something I won't forgive, Mr Savidge,' she said coldly.

He caught her arm in a light but determined grip and swung her round. 'Don't play the outraged innocent! We both know what you are!' he said savagely, tall frame tense. 'Do you want me to prove it?' Before she could protest or pull away, he bent his head and kissed her.

Her mouth quivered in shocked response to that dark current of desire, but every instinct protested at the primeval passion that ignored her right to choose whether or not to be kissed. Her reaction was just as primeval and just as passionate. Thrusting him away, she slapped him across the face, hard.

A muscle twitched in his lean cheek and his eyes narrowed. Catching her hard against him, he stamped kisses on her resisting mouth until she was breathless, weak with a wanting that she didn't dare to admit, and filled with mounting fury.

Senses swimming, she was terribly tempted to melt, to yield, to surrender to that storm of sensuality. But anger, born of pain, was even greater than the desire he evoked with his demanding mouth and body. She stopped pummelling his back and shoulders with angry fists and tugging at his black curls with furious fingers and briefly relaxed in his arms, realising that fighting him only fuelled that frightening force of passion.

As he lifted his dark head with the glint of triumph in his eyes, she wrenched herself free and slapped him again, so hard that his head jerked back.

Desire shocked to death by the violence of the blow and the look in her blazing eyes, Paul said grimly: 'Any man but me? Is that it?'

'Even if you were the last man in the world!' Lucilla rushed into the sanctuary of her flat and slammed the door. Leaning against the wooden panels, she buried her face in both hands, shuddering from head to foot.

She had never known the hot compulsion that could sweep man and woman into each other's arms without a thought for anything but the magic of the moment. Now, fired by his kisses, his powerful and urgent maleness, she was consumed with a longing that pulsated like liquid fire throughout her body. Her heart hammering painfully in her breast, she fought the crazy impulse to throw open the door and admit him to her arms and, inevitably, to her bed.

She wanted him so much. She wanted to lie in his arms and drown in the deep, dark waters of a mutual and heady desire. Most of all, she wanted to spend the rest of her life with him, she admitted on a sudden, choking rush of emotion.

He had quickened her to a fierce intensity of longing with those bruising kisses, that crushing embrace and the thrust of his urgent body. He had also shocked her into the realisation that she was deeply, irrevocably and quite hopelessly in love with him.

And she didn't know what to do about it . . .

After a disturbed night, a heavy-eyed Lucilla made her way to the hospital with a very natural reluctance to come face to face with the SSO.

She was greeted with evident relief by the night Theatre Sister. 'Am I glad to see you! I'm longing for supper and my bed!' Muriel Fletcher declared with feeling.

'Have you had a busy night?' Lucilla asked the question absently, her mind on Paul. She had just seen the surgeon in crumpled tunic and trousers, mask about his neck and black curls tousled as if he had pulled off a theatre cap with an impatient hand.

Surprised he had made such an early start to the day, Lucilla had steeled herself, but he had passed her without a word. She doubted he had even seen her as he strode down the corridor, staring straight ahead, lines of weariness etched into his handsome face. Perhaps he had suffered a virtually sleepless night too—and so he *ought*, she thought crossly, hardening the heart which had foolishly melted at sight of him.

Love him? Of course she didn't love him! She must have been feeling the effects of that last Martini to have given rein to such a crazy flight of fancy, she told herself sternly, having spent much of the night in ridiculing the idea and reminding herself of all the very good reasons why she couldn't possibly be in love with Paul Savidge.

'I suppose you slept through the storm!'

'Not entirely,' she said dryly. Together with the persistent thought of Paul, violent claps of thunder and the bright zig-zag of lightning and the sound of torrential rain had kept her awake. 'It was bad at times, wasn't it?'

'Very bad. Caused a lot of damage locally, and the cliffs subsided further down the coast due to the heavy rain. A house was struck and a tree crashed down on a car, killing the driver and injuring two people who were in the back. Several others were hurt in a pile-up on the motorway due to the flooding. A & E have been rushed off their feet and so have we! One man with a head injury is still in the theatre.'

'It sounds as if you haven't had a second to spare,' Lucilla sympathised. 'When did the SSO come in?'

'Oh, about three. He was called to one of his post-ops who was haemorrhaging. He decided to bring her back to theatre for investigation and she arrested on the table.'

'Oh, no!' Lucilla's heart sank. No wonder Paul had passed her like a man in a dream! A bad dream, she thought unhappily, for no surgeon liked to lose a patient in the theatre and have to face the subsequent inquiry.

'Paul managed to resuscitate, but it was a near thing. He was marvellous, just wouldn't give up,' Muriel said warmly. 'We tried everything—fibrillation, coramine,

the lot! But it seemed to be a lost cause until Paul opened
up the chest wall and hand-massaged the heart. That did
the trick, thank goodness! I swear he *willed* that woman
to live.' She yawned and stretched, bone-weary, then
got to her feet. 'She's in ICU, anyway. Paul's just gone
along to have another look at her. You must have passed
him in the corridor.'

'Yes, I saw him. I thought he looked very tired,'
Lucilla said carefully, trying to sound impersonal.

'He *is* tired. We had three emergencies, one after the
other—a thoracotomy, a splenectomy and a ruptured
appendix, and he chose to do them all rather than
overload the duty surgeon.'

'That sounds just like him . . .'

Muriel nodded. 'Conscientious, hard-working and
clever—*and* a thoroughly nice guy,' she approved. She
looked keenly at Lucilla. 'But I hear that you don't get
on with him.'

She smiled. 'Call it a power struggle. We have different ideas on how to run the unit,' she said lightly. 'I'm
Hartlake, he's Benedict's, and never the twain shall
meet!'

'I expect some of your nurses have already lost their
hearts to him.'

'A few, I daresay.' Drawing the duty book towards
her as her colleague went away, Lucilla ran through the
account of the busy night in Muriel's neat hand, but
the words blurred as she thought of her own foolish
readiness to lose her heart to the SSO.

Making her usual round of the unit, she found one
theatre still in use by the neuro-surgeon, who was operating on the serious head injury from the motorway
pile-up, and that another theatre was being prepared for
a pelvis dislocation from the same incident. It was no
wonder she was so terrified of driving, Lucilla thought
heavily. She might have overcome the fear by this time if

she hadn't seen the results of so many road accidents on the wards and in Theatres.

She was in her office, finishing off some paper-work before scrubbing to assist Paul with a radical mastectomy, when Julie walked in.

'Paul wants me to help him this morning, Lucilla. Is that okay? You've put your name on the theatre list.'

'I'm only too thankful if he wants your hands rather than mine,' Lucilla assured her brightly, torn between relief and chagrin, for she had been looking forward to another chance to prove that she wasn't entirely useless in the theatre, reluctant though she was to face the surgeon.

'Sure you don't mind?' Julie had known her long enough to see through the sparkle in her smile.

'Not in the least.'

'You might even be relieved! Laurie says Paul was in a foul mood yesterday and that you bore the brunt of his temper.' As a friend, Julie was more concerned than curious.

'No more than anyone else.' Lucilla didn't want it supposed or said that she'd been singled out for special treatment. 'He was beastly to everyone. He flattened Laurie and insulted Neil and reduced most of the juniors to nervous wrecks with his scowls and growls. The man's an arrogant, ill-tempered brute, and I wish to heaven I didn't have to work with him!' All her hurt and dismay and despair spilled over into the last, heartfelt words.

Julie stared at her friend in astonishment.

'Well, Nurse? Are you scrubbing for me or not?' Paul demanded impatiently from the doorway.

The staff nurse turned with such a guilty start that the suspicion that he was the brute under discussion was instantly confirmed. Eyes hardening to chips of black ice, he looked beyond Julie Whitfield to the bowed head of the Theatre Sister, who had promptly begun to be busy with a pile of forms, a betraying warmth in her face.

'No problem,' Julie sang out brightly. 'I'll have everything ready for you in no time . . .' With the flash of a smile that embraced both Sister and surgeon, she hurried away.

Paul studied the silent Lucilla, bitterly comparing the unit and its old-fashioned structure and its incompetent Theatre Sister with everything that he'd known before he came to Camhurst. The General was a good hospital of its kind; it wasn't and never could be Benedict's! Certainly not while the stubborn, spirited and much too lax Lucilla Flint was Sister Theatres. There were days when he looked on his new job as a kind of penance for his sins, he thought morosely.

Yesterday, for instance.

He'd been out of temper and short on patience and he had vented much of his fury and frustration on the Theatre Sister. Later, like a fool, he'd allowed the surging desire for the girl to take command.

He'd behaved badly. But it didn't justify that scathing criticism of him to her friend, he thought angrily. Good Theatre Sisters maintained the polite fiction that senior surgeons were minor gods if only for the sake of good working relationships.

The way that Lucilla Flint felt about him was abundantly clear. There had been no need for her to spell it out for the benefit of her nurses.

CHAPTER TEN

LUCILLA looked up, her attention compelled by the silent, seething scrutiny. 'Do you want something, Mr Savidge?' she asked, ice tinkling in her tone. He had no right to anger. *She* was the injured party!

'A private word, Sister.' Paul closed the office door with a snap.

She regarded the surgeon with wary eyes and a nervous leap of her heart as he advanced towards her with purposeful stride. 'I'm really very busy just now . . .'

'This won't take long.' His muscular hands took the weight of his powerful frame as he leaned on her desk, eyes narrowed to glare into her own, a pulse throbbing in the cheek with its pale hint of a bruise.

'Very well.' Lucilla looked at his hands and thought of their skill with a scalpel and the half tender, half angry touch that had swept a tear from her cheek and the never-to-be delight of knowing them reach out to her for all the right reasons. She loved his hands.

'There *is* something you can do for me,' Paul said grimly.

Putting down her pen, she raised her eyes to his face, so handsome and so dear despite its forbidding glower. She loved his lean, intelligent face with its laughter-crinkled eyes and the warm mouth that was forever promising to smile and failing to do so for her.

'Yes?' The brisk tone betrayed none of her heaviness of heart at the sound of hate in his voice. She loved his deep voice with the exciting timbre that sent shivers down her spine even when it cut her with cold contempt

or bruised her with savage mockery.

She loved him. With all her heart . . .

'You can remember my position as SSO in this unit and refrain from undermining my right to respect from your nurses!'

Her chin shot up. 'Don't you think you undermined *my* right to respect as well as my authority by speaking to me as you did yesterday—in front of several of my nurses!' she retorted proudly.

His eyes narrowed. 'I'll admit to that. It was wrong, and I apologise . . .'

Lucilla brushed aside the impatient words that seemed to her to hold no trace of regret. 'Perhaps it's different at Benedict's, but I'm used to good manners and pleasant attitudes from the surgeons in this unit, Mr Savidge. We all try to get on with each other—which is more than I can say for you! Ever since you arrived, you seem to have gone out of your way to upset people. You should have stayed at Benedict's where half the staff probably don't know the other half and personal feelings aren't so involved!' She was thankful as she spoke that he couldn't know just how deeply *her* feelings were involved, in fact.

'You wouldn't last five minutes at Benedict's,' Paul told her brutally, stiff with anger at the rebuke of words and tone. 'You've no idea of discipline and your work in the theatre is no better than average—and that's being kind!'

'Oh, don't bother to spare my feelings! I know just what you think of my work—*and* me!' Lucilla retorted hotly, flushed with hurt and temper. 'You've made it very plain—in more ways than one!'

'Not without good reason!'

'I think you're the most unreasonable man I've met in my life!'

'As the study of my sex seems to be your life's work, I

imagine you're an authority on male behaviour,' he sneered.

The shrill sound of the telephone broke across a quarrel that was rapidly descending to adolescent level. A passing theatre porter paused to look through the glazed door, his attention attracted by the sound of voices unmistakably raised in anger. The rumble of trolley wheels in the corridor announced the arrival of a patient for surgery.

'I believe that must be your mastectomy patient, Mr Savidge,' Lucilla said stonily, reaching to silence the telephone with a trembling hand. 'Don't let me keep you . . .'

The surgeon looked as if there was a lot more he would like to say to her, none of it complimentary. Instead, he stalked from the room, bristling with anger and affront.

Lucilla sighed. She felt she would be walking a tight-rope across a dangerous abyss in the days ahead. For she would see far too much of Paul Savidge for peace of mind or physical comfort and, she feared, fall even deeper into love with him for no reason but destiny.

'Theatres . . . Sister Flint,' she said briskly into the telephone, recalled to her responsibilities by the persistent 'hello, hello' on the other end of the line, thrusting the surgeon from her mind with an effort.

For days they spoke to each other as little as possible. Paul was rigid and Lucilla was frigid. He wouldn't relent and she wouldn't melt, and neither of them would apologise. He was pleasant to everyone else, charming everyone else with the smile that banished the harshness from his handsome features. Punishing her, Lucilla thought wryly, but at least she no longer had to contend with the rumblings of discontent among the staff.

She went about her work as if nothing had happened,

but everyone suffered from her sudden insistence on improved efficiency. Lucilla knew nothing about Benedict's except its reputation, but she was determined to show a critical surgeon that the General could provide a theatre unit at least as good as any that the famous London hospital boasted.

She took the message that summoned Paul to the ICU and saw that he was grim and tight-lipped on his return. The efficient hospital telegraph had been before him with the news, and she sympathised with a caring and concerned surgeon who had worked so hard to save a patient's life.

She waylaid him in the corridor. 'I hear your pyelithotomy patient died, after all. I'm sorry.'

Paul looked at her as though he wasn't really seeing her. 'I expected it, Sister. My main concern was that we shouldn't lose her in the theatre,' he said curtly.

'I gather there was some brain damage.'

'A considerable amount of brain damage. The prognosis was poor, anyway.'

'Bad luck,' Lucilla commiserated.

Hearing the note of genuine sympathy, Paul was surprised by an impulse to confide in the Theatre Sister. But she had been closely involved with the initial surgery and might have to give evidence if the relatives insisted on an inquiry into the patient's death.

'Bad workmanship,' he corrected with a hint of the anger he always felt when a patient died unnecessarily. 'A ligature was improperly tied during the pyelithotomy and that caused the haemorrhaging. I suspect the patient had a cerebral thrombosis, but the post-mortem will show what actually happened, I expect.'

Lucilla looked up at him, troubled. 'Neil's workmanship?' she ventured.

'I'm not going to commit myself on that score, Sister,' Paul said firmly. 'He's a young man at the start of his career and he shows promise. I'm not prepared to cast doubts on his ability, on or off the record.'

'Which means you'll take full responsibility!'

'My shoulders are broad.' He shrugged as if to prove it. 'Ligatures do slip—for no obvious reason, sometimes. It's extremely rare to lose a patient as a result. There'll probably be an inquiry, of course. I'm very sorry for Mrs Bridger's family. I'm sorry it happened.'

Sensitive to the rue in his voice, Lucilla said impulsively: 'Did it happen to you before—something of the kind, I mean? Is that why you left Benedict's?' She saw his eyes harden and his face close against her questions. 'Oh, I shouldn't ask, I suppose! And you wouldn't tell *me*, anyway!'

Deeply ashamed of an error of judgment that had cost him a consultancy and changed the direction of his life so completely, very reluctant to discuss the incident, Paul nevertheless heard himself saying: 'The circumstances were different. The result was the same, unfortunately. I took a chance and operated on a patient with a heart condition. He died on the table.'

'Did you have a choice?' Lucilla asked quickly, knowing that there were times when a surgeon must operate against all the odds.

'The patient had a choice—chemotherapy or surgery. I talked him into having the operation, to his cost.'

'Might he have died anyway?'

'He might have had a few more years of reasonably good life!'

The harsh tone betrayed the pain that a dedicated and caring surgeon had felt at the loss of his patient. The heart that loved him so much ached to comfort him. 'You can't be sure of that, Paul. Don't be too hard on yourself. We all make mistakes,' Lucilla said quietly, unaware that she used his first name.

'Surgeons can't afford them,' he said brusquely, and strode away.

Lucilla went out with Evan again that weekend. Dis-appointed and discouraged by Paul's continuing cold-ness, she was seeing more of the gynaecological surgeon than was probably wise, gaining a kind of comfort from his company. He took her to Romany's for dinner. They were in the bar when a flash of bright colour caught her eye and, turning, she saw Sally Lloyd in the doorway, clinging to Paul's arm. The girl sparkled with obvious satisfaction in her attractive escort and in the picture she presented in the short-skirted scarlet frock that empha-sised every curve and showed off long, shapely legs. Her long blonde hair tumbled about her lovely, laughing face in careful confusion.

He looked very pleased with himself, Lucilla thought, sick with dismay that he was dating the wild, wilful girl. As Evan followed her glance, she saw that he was surprised. Recalling his protective attitude to his young cousin, she wondered if he disapproved too. Hadn't he once hinted at Paul's success with women?

Seeing them, Sally dragged Paul across the room, her face aglow. 'Darling, how lovely to see you!' she ex-claimed, swooping to bestow a kiss on Evan as he held out a hand in warm welcome. 'Even if you *are* with another woman! Is this my latest rival?' She flashed an impish smile at Lucilla.

Evan laughed. 'You know Lucy,' he said lightly.

'Do I? Oh yes, I remember . . . hi, Lucy! This is Paul. Dishy, isn't he?'

'We've met,' Lucilla said coolly, freezing the surgeon with the chill of her smile, aware that he was ill pleased as herself at the chance encounter. But Camhurst was a small town, and if he wanted to run around with the promiscuous Sally Lloyd, then he

should do it elsewhere, she thought crossly.

Paul looked back at her, hard-eyed. He knew she was frequently to be found in Evan's company off duty, of course. Just one of the half dozen men she dangled on her string, he thought angrily. It was the determination not to become one of that retinue that had led to going out with Sally, but he was already bored with her youth and frivolous attitudes and he suspected she found him disappointing.

'Aren't you a nurse?' Sally swept on gaily. 'Paul's a surgeon, so you've lots in common. Why don't we swop—and then I can have my lovely Evan back!' There was a wicked gleam in her smile as she snaked an arm about Evan's neck and rubbed his cheek with her own.

'Sister Flint seems perfectly content with the man she has, Sally. Apparently I can't say the same for you,' Paul drawled in mock reproach.

Sally giggled, unabashed.

'Unhand me, woman—and sit yourself down for a drink,' commanded Evan, signalling to a waiter.

'Only if you promise not to talk shop. It ruins my appetite!' Obediently, Sally withdrew her arm and slid on to the padded bench beside him.

Left with no choice, Paul took the seat next to Lucilla. It puzzled him that she was apparently *Lucy* to her friends these days, and he wondered when she had stopped being *Cilla*. When she left Greg Harman to make a new life for herself in a different part of the country? Or had it only been Greg's special name for her?

Silent while the others talked, Lucilla toyed with the stem of her glass with restless fingers. She was having trouble with the ache in her breast and the foolish tears that pricked at her eyes. For it hurt that Paul preferred a girl like Sally Lloyd to herself. Thank heavens he didn't know how much it hurt!

Stretching out a hand, she missed the edge of the table and her glass fell, splashing the bright red wine all over her white dress and Paul's light tan slacks. The hot blood stormed into her face.

'Oh, how *stupid* . . . ! I'm so *sorry* . . . !' Lucilla was upset about her dress, even more upset about his immaculate trousers.

'No harm done.' Taut with annoyance, Paul produced a snowy hanky and dabbed at the spreading stain on his thigh.

'But there is! How *could* I have been so clumsy!'

'Evan, have you been plying the poor girl with drink so you can have your wicked way with her later?' Sally demanded, mock-stern.

Evan grinned. 'Of course.' He twirled an imaginary moustache. 'Once aboard the lugger and the girl is mine!'

Lucilla scarcely heard the words that made light of the incident for her sake. 'I really *am* sorry, Paul,' she said earnestly, putting a hand on the surgeon's arm in her anxiety to convince him that she hadn't deliberately spilled her drink. He was always so ready to think the worst of her!

Briefly Paul covered her hand with his own. 'It doesn't matter, Lucilla. Forget it . . .'

Swept off to the powder room by a concerned Sally to do something about her dress, Lucilla was too upset to notice that comforting touch or the easy use of her name or his softened tone. It was only later that it struck her as untypical of the man who was always so formal and chilly whenever he spoke to her, on and off duty.

Holding the folds of her skirt under a tap, she ran cold water over the stain and then dried her dress under the warm-air blower. It wasn't quite as good as new when they went back to the men, but at least she presented a reasonably respectable appearance. As Paul rose at their approach, she saw with renewed dismay that his slacks were noticeably stained.

She tried to apologise again.

Again he brushed aside the regretful words. 'It's unimportant, Sister,' he said, so impatiently that Lucilla subsided into her seat without another word.

Moments later, Paul whisked Sally off to the restaurant.

'Shall we go in, too?' suggested Evan.

Lucilla's gaze was on the surgeon as he ushered Sally through the tables with an attentive hand at her elbow and a smile hovering as he bent his dark head to listen to what she was saying. 'I seem to have lost my appetite . . .'

'You *are* upset,' he teased gently.

She smiled ruefully. 'It was such a silly thing to do!'

'It was an accident. Put it out of your mind. I'm sure Paul has forgotten—and forgiven.'

'I'm sure he *hasn't*! He doesn't like me and I didn't endear myself by throwing wine all over him. He'll glower at me all evening.'

'We don't have to eat here,' Evan said with more understanding than she knew. 'How about a Chinese?'

Lucilla smiled at him in sudden gratitude. 'You know all my little weaknesses,' she said, forcing brightness into her tone.

'I think you could say that,' he agreed with a hint of wryness in his hazel eyes. 'Come on, I'll take you to Heaven's Door . . .'

It was the name of a local restaurant that Lucilla particularly liked, but it had a poignant ring for her that evening. She couldn't help wondering if she was destined to remain at heaven's door, knowing that happiness lay beyond and was for ever out of reach because she had fallen in love with the wrong man.

Life would be so easy and so comfortable if she loved Evan . . .

Lucilla was woken out of a deep sleep by the insistent ring of the doorbell. She opened an eye to peer at the bedside clock. Ten past two, middle of the night. She turned over and snuggled into her pillows again, anxious to recapture a delightful if unlikely dream.

The still-shrilling bell roused her to an abrupt realisation of what had woken her, and she scrambled out of bed in alarm. She was muddled with sleep, fumbling for the elusive tie of her robe, as she opened the door.

She looked so young, so vulnerable and so touchingly pretty that Paul ached to sweep her up and into his arms, to cradle her close to his heart, to kiss the sweet, tremulous mouth that was O-shaped in surprise at sight of him.

'I'm sorry to disturb you, Sister, Are you alone?'

'What . . . what is it? What do you want? Do you know what time it is?' Lucilla demanded indignantly, startled into full wakefulness by his presence on her doorstep, fully dressed and devouring her with the dark intensity of his gaze.

'Is Evan with you?' he repeated impatiently.

Stiff with outrage, she glared. 'No, he isn't!' She kept a hand on the door, ready to slam it shut if he ventured to put even one foot over her threshold.

Paul frowned. 'Sure about that? I thought . . .'

'I don't care what you thought!' Lucilla blazed, spitting fire. 'He isn't here!'

He swore with an exasperation that concealed the swamping relief. 'Just when we need all the hands we can get! There's been an accident at Lonsdales. The casualties are going to the General and we're needed urgently in Theatres. Dress as quickly as you can. 'I'll wait for you in the car.'

Training instantly took over, wiping out her resent-

ment of his tone and the too-easy assumption that Evan
habitually stayed the night in her flat. 'I'll be down in ten
minutes . . .'

Lucilla fled to the bathroom to sluice cold water over
her face to chase away the last vestiges of sleep. Then she
scrambled into some clothes, pulled a comb through her
curls and snatched up bag and keys. In less than the ten
minutes she'd promised, she was hurrying towards the
purring Lancia. She scarcely had time to fasten the
seat-belt before the car shot through the gates of Ashley
House and headed for the hospital.

Paul drove fast through the deserted streets, steering
the powerful car with sure hands on the wheel that
allayed her initial flicker of anxiety. She shot a glance at
him.

'Did Muriel Fletcher call?' she asked.

'She was just about to ring me. I called the unit when I
realised what must have happened. Saturday night is a
bad time for disasters, of course. It isn't always easy to
contact off-duty staff who might not be in their own
beds,' he said dryly. 'I wasn't sure if *you* were home, but
I told Muriel I'd rouse you and take you in with me if
possible.'

'What *has* happened? What kind of disaster?'

'An explosion of some kind. It's a chemical works,
isn't it? The blast shook the town and lit up the sky. I'm
surprised you didn't hear the bang—or the sirens.'

'I didn't hear a thing until the doorbell woke me. What
about casualties? Do we know how many?' Lucilla's
thoughts leaped ahead to the demands that would
probably be made on her and everyone else that night.

'Between thirty and forty. The dead caught the full
force of the blast. Some men are badly maimed and may
not even get to Theatres. We must do what we can for
the rest.' Paul turned to look at her. 'Thank God for
your experience! You aren't likely to flinch from the

kind of surgery we'll be handling tonight and much of tomorrow.'

It was the first praise to fall from lips that usually sneered at her incompetence and inefficiency, and Lucilla hoped she could live up to those confident words. It was true that she'd had plenty of experience of routine surgery, both major and minor, but few actual horrors had come her way in six years of nursing. Her vivid imagination shrank from a vision of horribly burned and mangled bodies, and a shudder rippled through her slight frame.

Paul wanted to stretch out a reassuring hand, guessing at her thoughts and feelings, but he quelled the impulse, convinced that his touch would be unwelcome. There were times when he tormented himself with the image of Lucilla in other men's arms, being kissed and caressed into eager surrender and responding with all the fire of her passionate nature. He lay awake, wanting and wondering just how and when and why she had become so dear, so desirable. Her angry rejection of him had made a painful and lasting impact on him. Cynics might declare that only his pride was hurt. Paul knew better.

That night, a new book by a favourite author had failed to capture his concentration. Even the music he loved, played softly, had been unable to drive the disturbing image of Lucilla and Evan from his mind or the ache from a heart that was close to capitulation.

Studying the night sky as sleep continued to elude him, a sky as black as his jealous despair, he had felt the rock of the explosion and seen the blaze of unholy light that lit up the town and heard the wail of a warning siren. Reaching for his clothes and the telephone at the same time, Paul was talking to Muriel Fletcher at the General as Camhurst began to resound with police and ambulance sirens.

Only an emergency could have taken him to Lucilla's

door in the middle of the night, and he had steeled himself to face Evan with equanimity. She saw too much of his friend for Paul to doubt their relationship, and he knew he had absolutely no right to protest. Loving her gave him no rights at all.

He glanced at her pale, pretty face. 'Feeling apprehensive, Sister?' He wondered if she knew that his stubborn insistence on formality was a defence.

'Just a little,' she admitted quietly.

Paul nodded. 'So am I. Oh, not for the same reasons, perhaps. A city surgeon deals with the results of violence of all kinds more often than his counterpart in the provinces. That doesn't mean we get hardened to tragedy or that we're confident of coping with everything that's thrown at us. Even the most experienced surgeon worries about making mistakes when he's under pressure. A scalpel might slip in a tired hand. Tired eyes might fail to spot a vital sign . . .' He broke off, shrugging. 'I don't know why I'm spelling out the dangers, Sister. You know them as well as I do!'

He had never seemed so relaxed, so ready to talk. Lucilla was so anxious to make the right responses that she said too brightly: 'Yes, I do—and it's my job to see that it doesn't happen. Nothing like that will happen while I'm around. You'll know when you're getting dangerously overtired. *I'll* know—and I'll see to it that you take a break.'

'Your concern does you credit, seeing that we both know how glad you'd be to see the back of me,' he drawled, thinking her insincere.

Lucilla shot back into her shell. 'Nothing personal,' she said coldly. 'I'd be just as protective of any surgeon whose mistakes threatened my job and the unit's reputation.'

'The unit—yes, I'd forgotten it's your first love . . . if not the only one.'

Her face burned at the implication of the words. 'I wish you'd keep your nasty insinuations to yourself!' she snapped, turning her shoulder to him. She stared at the dark shape of houses and shops as they neared the hospital, hurt. Nothing had changed. He still couldn't speak to her without sneering. He had led her into betraying an interest in what happened to him and then mocked her concern. He was quite impossible to like!

Lucilla wished he had been just as impossible to love . . .

CHAPTER ELEVEN

THE HOSPITAL was a blaze of light and a flurry of ordered activity as a convoy of ambulances ferried the injured night shift workers from Lonsdales to the Accident and Emergency Department where a hastily-assembled team of doctors assessed their injuries and assigned them to wards or Theatres.

As Paul brought his car to a halt, Lucilla was out and heading for the entrance. By-passing the lift which was bound to be in use, she mounted the stone stairs to reach the top floor and the unit just as Paul emerged from the newly-arrived lift.

He raised a disapproving eyebrow at her slightly breathless state. 'What did you prove, Sister? How fit you are? Rushing off like that didn't save a second, did it? You should have taken the lift and conserved your energy.'

'Sparring with you takes up more of my energy than a few stairs,' she returned tartly as he held open the swing doors for her to pass through.

Paul looked down at the slender girl in the colourful skirt and sweater, looking so unlike the efficient Theatre Sister that she did her best to be, red-gold curls framing a lovely face that was flushed with exertion and indignation. His heart welled unexpectedly as he met the spirited challenge of her grey eyes. It wasn't the right moment or the right surroundings to admit how deeply he cared for her, even to himself, but it seemed that love chose when and where to declare itself.

'You're too quick to take offence,' he said mildly,

needing time to marshal his emotions, overwhelming in their intensity.

Lucilla stopped short, glowering. 'And you're always so quick to give it—at every opportunity! I've never known anyone so unfair, so unreasonable . . .'

'*Unreasonable!*' Paul exploded into an anger that was fuelled by the reluctant love and longing for this woman of all women. 'I've good reason to resent someone who was partly to blame for my cousin's suicide!'

'That's a very unforgiving attitude,' Lucilla accused hotly, forgetting how hard she found it to forgive herself. 'It's three *years*!'

'I know to the day just how long it is, Sister.' He lashed her to punish himself for the folly of loving her. He didn't want to be angry, to quarrel. He wanted to take her into his arms . . .

'Do you think I *don't*?' she demanded bitterly. 'Do you think I haven't lived with regret for three years —*and* guilt! I *liked* Pam. I trusted *Greg*! Most of all, I love my sister, and I don't know if I'll ever see her again! But you don't give a damn for my feelings, do you?'

'This isn't the time or the place to discuss them,' Paul said harshly, cutting across the words that had scarcely registered as his mind turned to the bustle of the unit and the demands of his job.

Lucilla looked beyond him to the group of green-clad figures bent over a patient wrapped in blankets, an intravenous drip attached to the trolley mast. Porters were manoeuvring another trolley out of the lift that connected directly with A & E, the accompanying nurse looking anxious as she monitored the patient's pulse. A theatre technician trundled oxygen cylinders into an operating room and a nurse sped from clinical room to scrub annexe with a covered tray.

Both surgeon and Theatre Sister knew that the picture told only part of the story. Behind the scenes, their colleagues were busily repairing torn and damaged flesh and tissue, stemming the flow of blood from ruptured arteries, setting broken bones, working to restore health and mobility and maybe life to those injured in the traumatic accident.

Private quarrels faded into insignificance in the face of tragedy on such a scale . . .

'No—but we've got to talk it out,' Lucilla insisted, heart thudding with the fear that the days only drove them farther apart instead of bringing them closer. 'We fight all the time, and I hate it, Paul! I want us to be friends.' It was impulsive, a cry from the heart.

His dark eyes were enigmatic. 'I wish it was possible . . . *Cilla*.' In an effort to make her understand the feelings that must always keep him from committing himself openly to friendship or anything more, he deliberately used the shortened version of her name that Pam had written in her despairing note before she took the overdose that killed her. It had been indelibly printed on his memory since the inquest. He didn't wait for her reaction, striding off to get into greens as the urgency in the unit intensified with the arrival of yet another patient.

Lucilla's eyes widened. '*I'm* not Cilla. You've mixed us up!' she called after him desperately, but the words that might have checked the surgeon in mid-stride were drowned by the loud hiss of the autoclave in the nearby clinical room.

Paul disappeared into the changing-room and she hurried to silence the temperamental sterilising equipment, impatient that it had chosen just that moment to misbehave but thankful that now she knew the real reason for Paul's hostility she could do something about it.

It was an easily understood mistake, she admitted. How could he know that Lucilla had been Lucy and

Priscilla had been Cilla from babyhood, their names being so ridiculously similar? She only had to convince him that he'd confused her with her twin and all would be well!

On that optimistic note, she went to change into her own theatre garb before checking on the situation and the state of the operating theatres.

There was no time to think about the absurd mix-up or even to mention it that night. Nor did Lucilla have time to be appalled by the extent or the kind of injuries that were brought into Theatres as men were extricated from the pile of rubble that had once been a chemical factory.

Pushing personal thoughts and feelings out of mind and heart, she worked beside Paul through the night and well into the next day, handing and holding instruments, tying ligatures, swabbing and sewing as he instructed and doing much of the work of an assisting surgeon. All the theatres were in use and off-duty nurses had been called in to provide an essential back-up for the surgeons, ensuring a supply of instruments and suture packs and dressings, fresh gowns and gloves, clean and tidy operating-rooms.

Some of the injured were close to death on arrival and all Paul's skill and determined efforts failed to save them. He worked like a tireless Trojan on those he could help, and Lucilla's admiration soared sky-high as she watched the sure hands at the delicate work of clearing the debris of clotted blood and damaged tissue, repairing or removing shattered organs, setting broken bones and sewing torn flesh. He was so clever, so patient, so *caring*, she thought warmly.

An elderly porter helped her and another nurse to transfer an unconscious patient from table to trolley at the end of surgery that had undoubtedly saved another life.

'I'd have sworn this one was a goner, Sister,' he

avowed. 'That Mr Savidge is a marvel, if you ask me!'

Lucilla's heart swelled with as much pride as if she was personally responsible for Paul's skilled hands and total dedication. 'Yes, we're very lucky to have him,' she said, looking after the surgeon with glowing eyes as he went into the annexe to change his stained gown and snatch a much-needed cup of coffee.

She was determined to carry on as long as he did, even at the risk of falling asleep on her feet. Like everyone else, she kept going on coffee and the occasional half sandwich and adrenalin. Working with Paul, she felt she earned his respect for her own efforts, and she was content with the nod of approval, the half-smile in dark eyes above the mask, whenever she anticipated a requirement or her hands were particularly deft.

Several hours later she was desperately tired, hot, thirsty and nauseated by the sights and smells of surgery. She loved theatre work, but one could have too much of a good thing, she thought, aching with weariness.

Paul was flagging too. At first, he had talked to her about each man and his injuries and chance of recovery, but as the hours passed and he needed all his energy and concentration for his work, he had spoken less and less. Now he opened his mouth only to specify an instrument or to give an instruction. His deep voice was firm and his hands were still rock-like in their steadiness, but Lucilla saw strain in his eyes and knew he must ache as she did. She was beginning to feel like an automaton with aching back and legs, cramp in her hands and a band of pain about her head.

As the latest of a long line of patients was taken away to an already overcrowded Recovery Room, she went to the telephone with a purposeful air. Then she followed Paul into the annexe. He had pulled off the bloodied gown and dumped it in the dirty bin. His discarded cap lay on the floor and he was bent over a basin, sluicing cold water over his head, muscles rippling in back and shoulders and bare arms.

The weary Theatre Sister longed to crawl into those arms and feel them close about her as she yielded to the overwhelming need for sleep. Instead, she put a towel into his groping hand as he surfaced, blinking wetly.

'Isn't it time you let someone else take over?' she said firmly. 'You've worked for nearly twelve hours with scarcely a break.'

'So long? I seem to have lost track of time.' Paul vigorously towelled his wet head to stave off the wave of weariness. The past hours had left no time to think about himself or anything else, but now he realised that head and eyes and limbs ached and that he was tense with tiredness. 'I'll just see to the next fellow and then perhaps I'll rest for an hour or so. He's the last of the urgent cases, isn't he?'

'Yes, I think so. Obviously we shall be busy for some time yet with the lesser casualties, but the pressure's off and you've done more than enough. In fact, you've performed a few miracles!'

'I don't know about miracles. I'm just doing my job,' he said impatiently, shrugging off praise.

'And doing it incredibly well.' Lucilla smiled at him warmly.

It was even harder to resist that sunny smile, the lure of her loveliness, when he was dog-tired. 'You need to rest more than I do.' Paul crumpled the towel and tossed it into the bin. 'I'm used to long stints in the theatre. Benedict's is an excellent training ground for all kinds of emergencies.'

'So is Hartlake!' she returned promptly, loyally, and instantly regretted the retort. Neither of them needed the reminder, she thought wryly.

Paul crushed the resentment that stirred anew at the

thought of her and Greg Harman and what their apparently short-lived affair had done to Pam. Maybe she had her own regrets, he thought charitably, seeing the shadow that touched her pretty face.

'I'm sure it is—and I'm filled with admiration for the Hartlake nurse I've had at my side all night,' he said generously. He regarded her with a slight smile and tucked a straying curl beneath her cap with gentle fingers. 'But even such a dedicated Nightingale needs to rest, Sister. Go home and get some sleep.'

Lucilla's stomach churned at his touch, the hint of a smile in those dark eyes caught at her heart and she was grateful for the tender tone that seemed to turn the formal address into near-endearment. Was he warming to her at last? There was nothing like working together in an emergency to create a kind of closeness between surgeon and scrub nurse, she thought thankfully, knowing that at times their minds and hands had worked in perfect accord.

'Only if you do!' she declared. 'I think you desperately need to rest. I think you're too tired to go on.'

'Yes, I'm tired, dammit! But I'm nowhere near being a danger to my patients!' Paul exploded, thrusting both arms into a clean gown. 'Tell them to wheel in the patient and I'll get on with what needs to be done, Sister!'

He snapped with an exasperation born of weariness and a stubborn dedication to what he saw as his duty, she realised. As he headed for the operating theatre with a jut to his jaw, she barred his way.

'I'm sorry—I'm not allowing you to work on. I've spoken to Neil Clifton and he's on his way to take over from you,' she said on a note of finality. She knew he wouldn't be pleased that she'd taken matters into her own hands. But even if she was officially off duty, she was still Sister Theatres and it was her responsibility to safeguard the patients and protect the surgeons from their willingness to work until they dropped.

Paul scowled furiously. 'Damn you, Lucilla! You had no right to do that without consulting me!' He didn't like his decisions made for him, even with the best of intentions.

'You said yourself that he's a competent surgeon. He'll be here in a few minutes.' Lucilla stood her ground in the face of an anger that was threatening to erupt over her head.

'I'm not arguing his ability. I'm questioning your high-handed interference!'

'You left Benedict's because something went wrong for you! I won't let you risk it happening again because you're too tired to think straight and too stubborn to be told. You're a wonderful surgeon and we don't want to lose you!'

Paul's eyes darkened. He had made a wrong decision rather than a slip of his surgeon's knife, but the patient had died, nevertheless. At the time, it had seemed like the end of his world. Now he wondered if destiny had dictated the turn of events—for coming to Camhurst to work at the General meant that he had met and loved the pretty, spirited girl who seemed hell-bent on telling him what to do!

'Save your lectures, Sister! I'm not one of your student nurses!' he snapped.

'I don't mean to lecture you.' Lucilla sighed over his wilful refusal to realise that she was motivated by loving concern for him. 'I'm only reminding you of what we talked about on our way here last night—was it only last night? You were worried about getting overtired and perhaps making mistakes. I promised I'd do my best to see that it didn't happen, and that's just what I'm doing.' She was so drained, physically and emotionally, that it took real effort to persist, but she was convinced that she was right. Tears suddenly sprang to her eyes, a weakness that she couldn't help. '*Please*, Paul!'

He didn't know if it was the seemingly genuine concern in those warm grey eyes or the way she said his name, but his anger slid away.

He capitulated. 'Very well, have it your way this time, as you've already alerted Clifton. But don't go over my head again.' He pulled off his gown. 'Go and get changed. If I have to go home to get some sleep then so have you!'

Having handed over her own rôle to the recently arrived Julie, Lucilla sped to the changing-room to take off her greens and shake her hair free of the confining mob-cap. A quick shower washed away some of the aching weariness of bone and muscle and the cling of ether that had begun to make her feel slightly sick. Almost asleep on her feet, she was thankful that she didn't have to wait for a bus or telephone for a taxi. Paul might be annoyed with her, but he wouldn't abandon her after all they'd been through that night, she knew.

He was in the Lancia, dark head bowed over arms folded across the steering wheel, and Lucilla's heart contracted with concern for the tired surgeon as she got in beside him and stowed her capacious bag at her feet.

Paul lifted his head to look at her. She smiled at him so warmly that it triggered the ache for her that was rapidly becoming intolerable. The longing to take her into his arms, to cover her mouth with kisses, to feel her body pressed close to him, to possess her—willing or not! —was almost too much for him in that moment when exhaustion combined with his heart's hunger and his body's need to make him vulnerable.

He straightened in his seat, fighting temptation, putting up the barriers that protected his pride even if his heart was irrevocably lost. 'What the devil kept you?' he demanded brusquely.

Lucilla's heart plunged with dismay. The closeness of the night's work was obviously at an end. He had gone back to detesting her. She didn't think she could bear it . . .

'Sorry! But you didn't have to hang around to take me home!' she retorted proudly. 'I can take care of myself!'

Paul admired that independent spirit—but there were times when he could shake her for it! In silence, he switched on the ignition and set the car in motion.

Lucilla nursed her indignation for a few moments, but she was too tired to sustain it. She glanced at him. 'Still furious with me, aren't you? For making you stop work?'

Paul shrugged. 'You were right. It *was* time to hand over before I put patients at risk.'

'Knowing I was right doesn't make it any easier,' she murmured shrewdly, sensing his stubborn pride.

She was so lovely, so dear to him, that it was too much of an effort to maintain the protective defence. 'I hate bossy women,' he said. But he said it with the ghost of a smile.

'Oh, so do I!' Lucilla agreed promptly. 'When I was training, I vowed I wouldn't turn into a sour, sharp-tongued autocrat that no one could get along with if I ever got to be a Sister!'

'Let yourself down, didn't you?' drawled Paul.

It was straight-faced, but Lucilla saw the twitch of his mouth and the hint of humour in his expression and knew he was teasing her. She didn't mind. It seemed the first real sign of a thaw in their relationship, giving new hope to the heart that loved him.

'I'm always breaking resolutions,' she said on a mock sigh. *Such as the one not to love you*, she almost added on an impulsive burst of honesty.

Her hands lay in her lap, slender and small-boned and seeming too fragile and delicate for all the capable work that they achieved in the operating theatre. Paul covered

them with one of his strong, surgeon's hands in a clasp
that was more of a caress. Lucilla tensed at his touch, felt
her heart tilt and her stomach muscles tighten, didn't
dare to look at him for fear he would read in her eyes all
that she hid away in her heart. He didn't say anything,
nor did she. Words didn't seem to be necessary. The
offer of friendship and its tacit acceptance was enough.

Paul returned his hand to the steering wheel. Sitting
by his side as he drove through the town on that hot, still
Sunday, lulled by the warmth and the smooth motion of
the car, Lucilla's eyelids began to droop.

Paul headed for the high, clean air of the Downs
instead of the tree-lined avenue on the outskirts of the
town and he slowed the car to a crawl as Lucilla slept
beside him. He turned his head to look at the pretty face
with its smudges of weariness beneath closed eyes, the
long sweep of thick, gold-tipped lashes on pale cheeks,
the sweetness of her mouth in repose.

He had never wanted to love her. Loving her, he had
never intended her to know it. Now, he felt he must have
one brief, memorable hour with her, away from everything that reminded them both of an incident in the past
that had affected both their lives. Perhaps for that short
time he could forget that she wasn't the sweet and lovely
and pure-hearted girl he wanted her to be . . .

Her relaxed body shifted with the movement of the
car as he turned a corner and her head came to rest
against his shoulder. She seemed so slight and so frail
that Paul marvelled at the unsuspected stamina that had
kept her going for those long and exhausting hours in the
theatre. She had met every demand without falter or
complaint, kept everyone else severely on their toes and
matched his efforts with her own in a way that commanded his admiration as much as his steadily growing love.

She didn't stir when he brought the car to a halt on the
rough grass of a cliff height overlooking the sea, some

miles down the coast from Camhurst. Paul half turned in
his seat, his heart wrenching with desire and so much
more. He was a passionate man and a naturally impatient one. Wanting Lucilla had been hard enough
even before he knew that he loved her too. He bent his
head to brush her lips with his own, very lightly. Her
eyelids quivered but didn't lift. Paul placed a hand along
her cheek in a loving touch and she sighed softly in her
sleep. He touched his lips to the corner of her mouth and
slid a gentle hand through her curls to cradle the bright
head. Lucilla murmured and turned her face to him like
a trusting child.

Not knowing if she was awake or still asleep, Paul
looked down at the lovely, heart-shaped face, tender-
ness in his eyes and in the curve of his mouth. He kissed
her again, very softly, and she put an arm about his neck
in drowsy welcome, her lips trembling and parting on
another sigh as she kissed him back.

Lucilla was sure she was dreaming, but she didn't want
to wake . . . not just yet. There was the promise of
paradise in the pressure of his mouth, the caress of his
hand as it curved about her breast, the warmth of his
body as he gathered her close. It was a tender embrace
with only an unalarming hint of desire, and she nestled
against him, the leather of his jacket and the tang of his
after-shave and the still-new smell of the car's upholstery
mingling to create an evocative perfume that would
forever remind her of that magical moment.

His kiss deepened to explore the warm sweetness of
her mouth, and his expert touch quickened darting
flames of desire as strong fingers swept over her breast
and stroked the curve of hips and thigh.

Strongly aroused, all thoughts of sleep banished,
Lucilla sat up abruptly in his arms and looked about her
in astonishment at the expanse of cliff and sea and sky.

'Where are we?' she muttered.

'Almost the classic question.' He smiled. 'Don't you mean *"Where am I"*?'

She didn't smile. 'I thought you were taking me home.' He was so unpredictable. What had been in his mind when he headed for the cliffs instead of Ashley House?

'I will—soon. I thought we both needed some fresh air and a change of scenery. Besides, we need to talk, and this is a good place to do it.' He pulled her closer to him and kissed her with sudden, urgent passion.

'This is talking?' Lucilla asked breathlessly when she was able to surface from the deep waters of that kiss.

'When we talk, we fight. Which is better?' His warm lips traced the curve of her mouth.

'Oh, this . . .' she agreed weakly, and melted into the arms that she had so often ached to know about her.

CHAPTER TWELVE

LUCILLA could have stayed in his arms for the rest of her
life, quite happily. To please Paul, to make him happy,
she would give anything . . . her heart, her body, her
whole life!

But she was afraid he would sense only the tumult of
her longing and miss the love that lay behind it. She
didn't want to be taken and then tossed aside by a man
who only desired her for the moment. With all her heart
she wanted him to love her. As she loved him.

Reluctantly she drew herself from his arms. 'Can we
walk, Paul? Just for a few minutes. My head aches a
little . . .' She opened the car door, wondering if he
knew she needed to put distance between them while she
took firm hold of her runaway feelings.

Paul followed her across the uneven turf and caught at
her hand. 'Don't go near the edge,' he warned. 'It
doesn't look too safe.'

'It's a long way down.' Lucilla peered cautiously over
the cliff edge. 'Oh, look!' She pointed. 'That's the
harbour at Camsea . . . right over there! We're a long
way from anywhere, Paul!'

'Not really . . . about a mile from the main road, that's
all.'

She turned her back to the broad expanse of sea and
sky and looked at the deserted Downs, the rough track
that he had driven along to this point and, far in the
distance, the huddle of houses that was the beginning of
Camhurst.

'It *seems* a long way from anywhere,' she said
doubtfully.

Paul laughed. 'What's the matter? Don't you trust me?'

'It's a long walk if we end up quarrelling—and we usually do!' Lucilla reminded him ruefully.

'Then you'll have to be careful what you say to me, won't you, Sister?'

'*Me!* You're the one who . . .' Lucilla broke off as she saw the twinkle in his eyes. She smiled. 'You said you wanted to talk,' she prompted. Perhaps now was the time to sort things out, to straighten out the confusion, to pave the way to a relationship that was based on more than heady mutual desire, she thought hopefully.

Paul put an arm about her shoulders as they stood at the top of the cliffs with the seagulls wheeling overhead, filling the air with their piteous cries. 'Suddenly it isn't important,' he said quietly. 'Suddenly nothing matters but being with you, like this, away from everyone and everything. Talking can wait . . .' He bent his head to kiss her.

Lucilla clung for a long, breathless moment, then she pushed him away. 'I think we should go home,' she said firmly, unable to trust the flame that leaped to meet the passion in his tall, powerful frame.

'Your place or mine?' His attractive smile was reflected in the glowing dark blue eyes.

Lucilla had waited a long time for the warmth of that special smile, and its enchantment completed the assault on her heart that first meeting had begun. She knew she would love Paul until the end of time, come what may. But she wasn't ready to give her all in return for one smile and a handful of kisses!

She was swamped with yearning for the heaven she could know in his arms, and all the very good reasons that had kept her virgin in the face of past temptation seemed not to matter at all in the face of present loving and longing. But she didn't trust Paul. She was afraid he would take her and make her his own and then walk away like a man who had no heart to give.

For it certainly wasn't love that had compelled him to bring her to this isolated spot, high on the Downs, with only the seagulls to take an interest in them. It was sheer, unthinking passion that trembled on his lips and in his limbs as he kissed her and held her, filling him with an urgency that overcame everything else.

The dislike, the contempt, the anger that had sprung from a confusion of identity had all been very real, Lucilla knew. Yet he had forgotten those feelings in the heat of a desire that glowed so ardently and so persuasively in his smiling eyes.

'I intend to fall into bed and sleep the clock round,' she declared.

'I know the feeling. Your bed or mine?' Paul teased her gently, but there was a deep current of desire underlying the light words.

'You *are* an optimist!' Lucilla laughed at him, stifling the throb of her heart and the tug of her body's foolish weakness.

'You don't know how much I want you,' he said, his voice soft, urgent with longing.

It was so direct that the thrill of his deep voice and the burn in his eyes sent a shiver down her spine. She shook her head in quick, almost angry refusal. She didn't trust herself to speak. She couldn't say she didn't want him —it wasn't true, and she couldn't bring herself to lie to him. At the same time, it would be much too dangerous to admit to wanting him with all her heart and soul and body. So she said nothing, that abrupt negation saying it all for her.

Paul tensed with angry disappointment, trying to understand, trying to be patient, trying not to resent or remember the men she had allowed into her arms. One man in particular, with disastrous results . . .

'Any man but me!' he accused bitterly, the anger threatening to overwhelm every other feeling.

'That isn't so . . . !' Lucilla began to fume at his refusal to see her in anything but a bad light. She knew she had offended him with yet another rejection. One step forward, three steps back, she thought wearily, wondering if things would ever progress in the right direction for her happiness.

'That's the way it looks to me!'

'That's the way you want to see it! You've never been right about me since the day we met!'

'My dear girl, I knew exactly what you were long before I set eyes on you,' Paul sneered cruelly.

Anger soared. 'I doubt if you even knew I existed, you stupid, arrogant . . . *oh!*'

Paul stopped her mouth with his own, catching her so hard against him that her breasts felt bruised by the unexpected impact with his chest. His kiss was savage, sensual, fiercely demanding, overriding her stifled protest.

Lucilla was outraged by the entirely loveless passion that seemed to be so much stronger than his mistaken contempt for her. In a frenzy of fury, she tore herself out of his arms, pain radiating through her at his brutal, uncaring attitude.

He didn't think she merited either his respect or his consideration, damn him! He'd prejudged her because he thought she was Cilla, and nothing she had said or done since first meeting had changed his opinion of her in the slightest. Damn him! Damn him!

She threw herself at the man she loved, hammering at him with clenched fists, eyes blazing, so beside herself with hurt and temper that she didn't realise she was spitting and swearing like a vixen.

Taken aback by the sudden onslaught, Paul backed away from the spitfire of a Theatre Sister, torn between anger and amusement. Suddenly the ground beneath his feet slid away as a considerable chunk of cliff edge, weakened by the recent heavy rain, crumbled with his weight.

·Lucilla's blood ran cold as she stared in horror at the space where he had been standing . . .

She threw herself full-length on the rough ground without a thought for her own safety and peered over the edge, steeling herself for the sight of his shattered body on the beach a hundred feet below, her heart filled with dread. She'd killed him! She was a murderer! She had lost her temper and thrust Paul over the edge of the cliff, and she could never, ever live with herself again! She wanted to die too!

'*Paul!* Oh, God! Oh, my *love*, my dearest, *dearest* love! *Thank God . . . !*' The words tumbled headlong from her heart and tears streamed down her face as she saw him lying on a precarious ledge about twenty feet below her, his fall broken by the ancient stump of a tree—and *alive!*

'I'm all right, Lucilla—no bones broken. I've wrenched my back, that's all. Don't panic, there's a good girl. Just get some help, and be quick about it,' Paul urged, striving to sound calm although he was far from happy about his situation. At any moment, more of the cliff might collapse, taking him with it to the rocky stretch of shore that was a sheer drop from where he lay. The smallest movement could bring down the ledge that had saved him, he knew. 'I can't climb up because I don't trust the cliff—and I don't fancy the way down,' he added with a wry attempt at humour.

'Help . . . ?' The cool-headed Theatre Sister who always knew just what to do in an emergency and prided herself on coping with the most unexpected situation looked about her wildly at the empty sea and sky, the deserted beach, the rolling expanse of uninhabited

Downs and the distant houses. Her mind was a blank.

'Get to a phone . . . !'

'I don't want to leave you,' wailed Lucilla, sure he would plunge to his death the moment she turned her back.

'You've no choice!' he told her with a sudden impatience that snapped her out of her blind and helpless panic. 'Now get going . . . take the car!'

Scrambling to her feet, she ran across the clumpy turf towards the Lància. Without even thinking about it, she slid into the driving seat, thankful that he'd left the keys in the ignition and that it was an automatic transmission and that she'd recently re-learned the rudiments of driving at least. She didn't have time to remember her own fears. Paul's life was in danger, and that was all that mattered! She loved him and she couldn't bear to lose him! Somehow, she had to drive his powerful car to the nearest house or farm or pub or telephone box . . .

Lucilla never knew how she did it, but she was sweating and stumbling over her words and ashen-faced when she finally reached the main road and the blessed sight of a telephone box and managed to dial 999 with shaking fingers. As soon as she'd made clear the gravity of the situation and explained as well as she could the position where Paul was trapped on the crumbling cliff, she sank to the grass verge beside the telephone box and buried her face in her hands, overwhelmed with the sobbing that welled up from deep, deep down.

The drive had been a nightmare experience, bringing back all the trauma and terror of that childhood accident, the loss of her parents and small brother, the fear that had made her sick and trembling at the mere thought of being in control of a car—but she had done it! She had actually driven Paul's Lancia along that rough grass track to the main road and then almost a mile to the nearest telephone while other cars shot past her at speed, sounding their horns at the stupid woman driver who seemed to be all over the road.

She *couldn't* go back to the cliffs, even on foot. She *knew* it was too late. For all her efforts, Paul was now lying dead at the foot of the cliffs. His weight, the slightest movement, the crumbling state of the cliff itself—he'd never had a chance!

She cried and cried, shoulders shaking, slumped like a broken-hearted child on the grass verge, while the Lancia stood at the side of the road with its engine still running and its door wide open. The police car drew up a short distance from her, and soon a kindly policewoman had an arm about Lucilla's shoulders and was leading her towards the car.

She panicked, pulled away. 'Paul! I have to get to Paul . . . !'

'Nothing you can do, my dear. Everything's under control. The coastguard has been alerted and a helicopter is on its way to rescue your friend . . .'

'The car . . . it's Paul's car!' She looked back at the policeman who had switched off the engine and removed the keys and locked up the Lancia. 'I drove it here . . . I had to! But I don't have a licence—that's breaking the law, isn't it?' Still shocked by what had happened to Paul, still shaken by her need to use his car, she was distraught.

'I expect we'll overlook it in the circumstances,' the policewoman soothed. 'Matter of life and death, wasn't it—and no harm done that I can see.' She helped Lucilla into the back of the police car and got in beside her. 'They'll take your friend to the General, I expect. You say he isn't badly hurt? It might be a good idea to take you there too . . . let a doctor look at you. You've had a nasty experience . . .'

'It *was* an accident! I didn't *mean* it! Oh, God—I *love* him! Why would I want to hurt him!' Lucilla clutched at the girl's arm, desperate to be believed.

'No one's accused you of anything, dear . . .' The policewoman leaned forward to speak to her colleague. 'Have a word with HQ and see if there's any news. Those cliffs will have to be fenced off, I should think—before someone *is* killed!'

Listening, fresh tears streaming, Lucilla heard the report over the two-way radio that a man had been taken off the side of the cliff by helicopter and was on his way to hospital. The coastguard station had acted promptly and a helicopter had happened to be in the air over Camsea when the message came through. It had been the work of only minutes to head down-coast and locate Paul's prone figure and winch a man down to lift him to safety.

Back on familiar ground at the General, Lucilla pulled herself together. Over the worst of the shock and the terrible, tearing anxiety about Paul, she turned down a suggestion that she should be admitted for overnight rest and observation.

'The wards are full of more deserving cases,' she reminded the young Casualty Officer. 'There's nothing wrong with me, Derek. I'm just a bit shaken up, that's all. I just want to go home and crawl into bed and forget it ever happened.'

Nodding, he handed her some tablets. 'Very sensible. Take these now and they'll calm you down so that you can sleep. You're probably overtired, Lucy. I hear you had quite a night in Theatres.'

She grimaced. 'Yes . . . but it was nothing to the night you had down here!'

'It was pretty grim,' he agreed.

Lucilla hesitated and then plunged. 'How is Paul Savidge?'

'Oh, not too bad. We've X-rayed his back and there's no serious damage—just a few wrenched muscles.

We've sent him to a private ward for a few days' rest. He'll be back at work and as good as new by the end of the week.' If he was curious about the circumstances that had led to surgeon and Theatre Sister being on the cliffs beyond Camsea after a long stint in the operating theatre, it didn't show, and Lucilla was grateful. She knew there must be a certain amount of interest, but she couldn't face a barrage of questions just yet.

She didn't go to see Paul. She didn't think he would want to see her. She didn't believe he would ever forgive her for what she had done—and she couldn't bear to see the accusation and hatred in his dark eyes.

How could she hope to convince him that she hadn't meant him any harm when she'd flown at him like a fury and he didn't know that it was only because she loved him so much?

They'd been at loggerheads since the day they met. He had never had a good word to say for her, and he still didn't realise that she wasn't the Cilla Flint he felt he had good reason to loathe and despise.

Lucilla had some leave due, and Matron was very understanding when she asked if she could take it that week. She felt guilty about deserting her post when Theatres was extra busy, but she felt she'd reached the end of her tether. Falling in love with the SSO had taken its toll of her resources, she thought ruefully, mentally drafting her resignation because she didn't feel she could go on working with him in the circumstances.

'Don't be silly, Lucy! You saved his life, from all I hear!' Julie exclaimed when Lucilla said so to her friend, who had called at the flat on her way home, anxious about Lucilla's unexpected absence.

Needing desperately to confide in someone and knowing that Julie would never betray her secrets, Lucilla told her just what had happened. Like everyone else, Julie knew that rain had caused subsidence of the cliff edge where Paul had been standing on that Sunday afternoon and that he was lucky to be alive. Now she knew the full story.

'Thank heavens he wasn't killed!' she exclaimed.

'I thought I *had* killed him!' shuddered Lucilla. 'He said some horrid things and I flew at him, and the next thing I knew he'd gone over the edge!'

'Oh, poor Lucy! What a dreadful shock for you!' Julie put a comforting arm about her friend.

'I went completely to pieces,' Lucilla confessed wryly. 'Me—a product of Hartlake! I feel so ashamed!'

'Nonsense! You kept your head enough to drive his car, didn't you? No mean feat for someone who's never driven a car in her life,' Julie said stoutly. 'But I don't understand what you were doing on the cliffs after working all night. You live next door to each other—you didn't have to drive all that way for some privacy!'

'It wasn't my idea,' Lucilla said defensively. 'I fell asleep in the car and when I woke up, there we were! Miles from anywhere!'

'Did he wake you with a kiss, Sleeping Beauty?' Julie's eyes twinkled.

Lucilla was silent, but the rich, betraying colour swept into her face. Wisely, Julie didn't pursue the subject, recognising that her friend was deeply distressed. She worried about Lucy. Without saying anything all these weeks, she had watched a level-headed and lighthearted Theatre Sister lose her confidence and her sparkle, her interest and her delight in her job and her carefree attitude to life and loving. Julie had blamed Evan and his reluctance to commit himself. Now she wondered if she'd mistaken her man!

'Anyway, no more of this absurd talk of leaving,' she swept on firmly. 'What would the General do without you? Or any of us?'

'I can't work with Paul!'

'Then don't work with him,' Julie said sensibly. 'You managed to avoid it before and can do so again. I'll be his regular scrub nurse as long as I'm available. He was always satisfied with my work.'

'I dread seeing him. I don't think he'll even talk to me!'

'Nothing new in that, is there? You never did get on,' Julie reminded her lightly. 'It's become a standing joke among the staff. No one will think it odd if you aren't speaking.' She gave her a little hug. 'Look, you aren't up to making decisions at the moment, Lucy. You haven't had a break for months and now everything's got on top of you. Relax for the rest of the week and you'll feel much better when you come back to the unit, and everything will look different, I promise.'

'Yes, I expect you're right.' Lucilla found a smile for her. 'I'm making mountains out of molehills,' she said brightly, trying to sound like her old self even as she wondered if that former sunny, untroubled girl would ever surface again.

If this is love then I could have done without it, she thought wryly.

Paul returned to his flat before the end of the week, discharged as fit but warned not to indulge in any strenuous exercise for a few weeks. He was determined to return to work as soon as possible.

He didn't know what to do about Lucilla. He had expected her to visit him in the private wing. He had ached to see her and assure her that he didn't bear any grudge and that he knew it had been accidental and entirely his fault. But she hadn't shown her face or sent any message of regret or concern. It hurt him that she obviously cared so little. He was much too proud to show it.

He knew now if he hadn't known before that he was

never going to get close to Lucilla. He had no intention of courting yet another rejection. He had irrevocably lost his heart, but he wasn't going to throw his pride after it!

Paul stepped out of the lift just as Lucilla closed the door of her flat, going out to shop for the weekend food. The blood drained from her face and her heart seemed to stop at the sight of him. For a tense and timeless moment, they looked at each other.

Love and longing welled in her breast. 'You're home, then,' she said stiffly, wanting to throw her arms about him and cry out her relief and her need of him against that strong shoulder.

He was chilled by the coolness of her tone, the indifference in the lovely grey eyes. 'Yes.'

'I'm glad you're . . . all right.' Only the tiny break in her voice hinted at the tumult of her emotions. Her heart was hammering high in her throat. Her eyes felt gritty with tears she didn't dare to shed. She was flooded with a dreadful despair as she met the hard, unforgiving eyes. The gulf between them was greater than it had ever been, and it was all her fault!

The obvious insincerity of the words stabbed him. 'How are you?' Words were inadequate to bridge the icy chasm that stretched between them, Paul thought angrily, longing to hold her in his arms and know again the sweetness of her lips and the softness of her body against his own.

Loving her was hell with no promise of an end to it . . .

'Me? I'm fine!' It was a bright, deceptive lie.

I'm sorry! I'm sorry! I'm so sorry, her heart cried despairingly, but he couldn't hear that, could he?

Or surely he wouldn't turn away from her with that curt, indifferent nod and let himself into his flat without another word.

CHAPTER THIRTEEN

AT THE END of a busy week in Theatres, Lucilla was glad
to relax over a cup of coffee and a rare gossip with Julie
in her small sitting-room. She had spent the morning
assisting Paul with a cholecystectomy and a hernia repair
and, as always, working with him had drained her
emotions rather than taxed her ability. It had proved
impossible to avoid scrubbing for him entirely, but he
was so absorbed in his job that it was easy to believe she
was no more than an efficient pair of hands to him.

Julie was happily reciting all the symptoms that led her
to believe she might be pregnant at last when the SSO
put his dark head round the open door, looking fit and
tanned and very handsome in dark blue slacks and blazer
and rollneck sweater.

'I'm off now, Sister—I want to get in a round of golf
while the weather's on my side. Neil Clifton will take
over the rest of my list.'

The cool tone and the complete lack of a smile stabbed
Lucilla anew with the pain of being kept out of the life of
the man she loved. Ever since the cliffs incident and his
return to Theatres, Paul had spoken to her only as a
stranger and only when necessary. Now her heart contracted with the familiar love and longing that he never
seemed to sense and wouldn't welcome, anyway.

'Have a good game,' she said brightly, keeping up the
pretence that they were on reasonably good terms for
the sake of her pride. She had weathered the first
difficult days of working in an atmosphere of curious
speculation, and her cool composure had convinced
their colleagues that the circulating rumours about her

relationship with the SSO were unfounded in fact.

'Oh, I expect to lose—I'm no match for Evan. You'll know where to reach me if you need me . . .'

'We'll do our best to manage without you.' Lucilla's bright smile concealed the persistent ache in her heart.

Convinced that she was actually assuring him she could happily live without him in her life, Paul turned to Julie, whose bright eyes always sparkled for him. She was a very nice girl who had made him welcome in the days when Lucilla was showing him a very cold shoulder, and he saw understanding and warm sympathy now in the smile she sent him.

'It's the harbour race this weekend, isn't it? It sounds an event not to be missed. You'll have an excellent view of the proceedings from your cottage.'

The race was an annual event, a fun affair for charity, organised by the local Rotary Club and supported by the youth of the district. Small boats were decorated like carnival floats and the crews wore fancy dress, and local residents and holiday visitors flocked to watch the motley collection of vessels make their way across Camsea Harbour without the aid of sail or engine. It was a highlight of the summer season.

'Oh, we won't be watching!' Julie assured him gaily. 'We've entered for the race. It should be great fun as long as the boat doesn't sink! Keith says it's seaworthy now, but I'm not so sure! We're doing it up as a floating hospital ward and using bedpans for paddles, and I'm hoping Lucilla will be our Florence Nightingale. Can we rely on you to cheer us on? We'll need all the support we can get. Come to lunch,' she added generously.

'I wish you'd suggested it sooner! I've accepted an invitation to lunch with the Lloyds. I daresay you've heard that Sally is competing and that Evan is one of her crew? I gather they mean to fly the skull and crossbones and dress up as pirates.'

'What about you, Paul? You'd make a very convincing pirate with those flashing dark eyes and beautiful black curls,' teased Julie.

The surgeon smiled and shook his head. 'Beneath my dignity.'

'I mean to be a spectator too,' Lucilla said firmly. 'I've no desire for a ducking. I remember last year when half the competitors ended up in the sea!'

'But that's the fun of it!' Julie exclaimed. 'Non-swimmers aren't allowed to take part, so there's no danger and there's always someone handy to pull out those who do go into the water.'

Paul glanced at his watch. 'We might run into each other in Camsea, then, Sister,' he said as casually as if he wouldn't be straining his eyes for a sight of her. It was impossible for him to see Lucilla and work with her, day after day, and not fall deeper into love. But he could and did conceal his feelings with a cloak of indifference, while she continued to go out and about with Evan and other men and behave as though he would never mean anything to her.

'One never knows,' Lucilla agreed as carelessly as if she didn't wish with all her heart that he would bridge the terrible gulf between them with an offer to take her to watch the harbour race. One friendly word, one meaningful smile, was all that was needed to heal her heart and give her some small hope for the future. 'But we shall probably miss each other in the crowd. People come from miles around . . .'

As the surgeon went away without another word, Julie poured more coffee, shooting a sidelong glance at her friend. 'You'll never get anywhere if you continue to crush the poor man in that fashion,' she said bluntly.

'I don't know what you mean . . .'

'Yes, you do! He was angling to see you on Sunday and you knew it! You snubbed him mercilessly.'

Lucilla shrugged. If Paul *had* forgiven her and still wanted her in any way at all, he would be doing all he could to prove it, she felt. Instead he was cold and distant, never referring to his fall or what had led to it—and he was apparently still dating Sally Lloyd and seemed to be a welcome visitor to the girl's home. That fact spoke volumes, surely.

'If Paul Savidge wants to see me at any time he only has to take three steps across a landing and knock on my door,' she said tartly. 'You seem to have forgotten how he feels about me, Julie. Particularly since I pushed him over the cliff.'

Julie sighed. 'I wish you'd stop saying that, Lucy. You *didn't* push him over the cliff, and it sounds dreadful.'

'It *was* dreadful!'

'For him too! Such an awful experience ought to have brought you together. Whatever happened that afternoon that you can't even talk to each other, for heaven's sake?'

'I told you what happened.'

'He made a pass and you got annoyed. But what was so terrible about that? So he chose the wrong moment. Do you mean to hold it against him for ever?'

'You don't understand, Julie. He thinks I'm *Cilla*!'

Julie's brow wrinkled. 'Why does he?'

'I don't know, but he *does*! It was bad enough when I thought he disliked me because I'm Cilla's sister. Did I tell you Pam Harman was his cousin? He was very fond of her and he hates the girl who broke up her marriage. He thinks *I'm* that girl. He knows that Greg fell in love with a nurse called Flint who worked at Hartlake, but he doesn't seem to know that there were two of us!'

'Then *tell* him, idiot! Tell him he's got the wrong Nurse Flint! Anyone could make that mistake, Lucy.'

'He wouldn't believe me. No matter what I tried to tell him. He's made up his mind about me and that's it . . .'

'Nonsense! I suspect he'll be relieved and thankful to learn that you had nothing to do with Pam Harman's death. He has a very soft spot for you, Lucy.'

'Well, it certainly doesn't show!' Lucilla tried to keep the pain and the bitterness out of her voice.

'Paul isn't the type to parade it, is he? He's proud —and you aren't exactly encouraging,' Julie reminded her dryly. 'You treat him like a leper most of the time! When I think of the way you encourage some men who don't deserve it at all . . .'

'I don't encourage any of them in the way that sounds,' flared Lucilla. 'If you've said that kind of thing to Paul . . . ! You're as bad as he is! It's just the sort of thing he says about me. He thinks I'm a bed-hopper, and he's never forgiven me for not hopping into *his* bed!'

'Is that a fact? If I were single and he'd fancied me, I'd have hopped into his bed like a shot,' said Julie with cheerful frankness, hiding her surprise that there had been more to the relationship between new SSO and Sister Theatres than she'd ever known. 'So would plenty of other girls.'

Lucilla jumped up, overturning her coffee cup in her indignation. 'I daresay! But I don't regard it as any kind of a compliment, Julie! I know sex is the eighth wonder of the modern world, but I'm old-fashioned, and I happen to believe that love should come first!'

'And you're in love with Paul . . .' Alerted by the hot words, Julie wondered why she hadn't realised her friend's plight until that moment. But Lucilla was so level-headed, so dedicated to nursing, that she'd almost given up hope of seeing her fall in love at last. Besides, she had been deceived by the ongoing friendship with Evan, Lucy's constant talk of him and the many evenings they had spent together of late, into believing he was the one man who might eventually win her friend's heart. That apparent fondness for the gynae surgeon had probably misled a lot of people. Including the new SSO. 'Oh, dear!' she sighed.

'You see as clearly as I do how hopeless it all is, don't you?' Dejected, Lucilla sat down again. 'Paul isn't the kind who'd want to know about loving, is he?'

Julie didn't feel qualified to answer that question. 'What about Evan?' she fenced. 'People are saying you mean to marry him—you've seen so much of him lately.'

Lucilla shrugged. 'Camouflage.' Evan had been very good, very understanding, about allowing himself to be used. She didn't doubt that he understood the situation.

'Very clever! It didn't occur to you that Paul might also think you and Evan are heading for the altar?'

'I don't suppose he's interested.'

'I've never known you to be so defeatist,' Julie scolded sternly. 'Whenever you've wanted anything in the past you've thrown yourself heart and soul into getting it! Look how you worked for your badge. Made Nurse of the Year, didn't you? Look how hard you've worked at being a really good Sister Theatres. The unit is a credit to your efforts!'

'Those things were different,' Lucilla said wearily.

'How different? Both dear to your heart, weren't they? So is Paul, isn't he? If you *really* love him!'

'So I should throw myself at him, heart and soul?' Lucilla's smile was crooked. 'Don't be naïve, Julie. You know as well as I do that a man hates to be chased even by a woman he wants. He likes to make all the running.'

'It seems to me that Paul did some running and that you took fright and fled into Evan's arms,' Julie said shrewdly. 'What's the man to think, Lucy?'

'That I don't want him,' Lucilla admitted quietly.

Julie nodded. 'Exactly . . .'

As her friend went away to check on the progress of the patients in Recovery, Lucilla took a handful of paper tissues from a box and began to mop up the spilled

coffee. She was reminded of an evening when she had
spilled wine over Paul and herself. Accidents will happen—but her life had been a long chapter of disasters
since the arrival of a new SSO. There was no good
reason why her heart should be yet another casualty, she
suddenly determined.

She loved Paul with all her heart and she longed to
spend the rest of her life with him. But that would never
happen while they stood one on each side of a gulf of
misunderstanding and suspicion. Surely the sacrifice of
her pride was a small price to pay for a chance of
happiness.

I want you very much . . . Paul's words still echoed in
her head and her heart. Perhaps Julie was right. Perhaps
she *had* foolishly taken fright at a powerful sexuality that
had rocked her to the very foundations of her being. But
Paul's desire for her and her wholehearted response
might be the key to real and lasting happiness for them
both! Giving herself to him, in love and for his delight,
might create a bond that nothing could break and even
inspire his cold heart to warm to her . . .

Lucilla looked at her reflection in the dressing-table
mirror with a doubtful expression. Had she been too
heavy-handed with eye make-up and lipstick? Was it a
good idea to brush her curls almost out of existence and
sweep her hair high and sleek in faithful imitation of
another woman's sophisticated style? Was the filmy
chiffon dress too blatantly inviting in the way it clung to
her body?

Perhaps it was all a complete waste of time and
effort, anyway. Paul might not even come home that
evening . . .

She sped to the already open door of her flat at the
sound of the lift arriving at the third floor. Paul stepped
out of it, humping his golf clubs.

'Hi! How was your game?' Lucilla asked, too brightly, voice pitched too high. Her heart was thumping and she felt silk with nervous excitement.

'Pretty good.' Paul was ready to welcome an unexpected overture of friendliness until he realised that she had rushed out to meet someone else. Another man, obviously. She was dressed to kill and looking prettier than ever with that excited colour in her cheeks and a betraying sparkle in her grey eyes. He still couldn't get used to the jealousy that consumed him at the thought of her with any other man. He had no claim to Lucilla, but that didn't stop him loving her, wanting her, he thought heavily.

'Oh, good. It was a lovely afternoon for it too.' She detained him almost desperately with the warmth in her lilting voice. It was almost as effective as clutching at his arm. 'Why not drop off your clubs and come in for a drink, Paul?'

His eyes narrowed. 'You look as if you're ready to go out for the evening.'

'Do I? In this old thing! Good heavens!' She flicked the folds of a specially bought dress in laughing disdain. 'No, I'm not going anywhere. How about you?' Her sudden smile was brilliant if shaky. 'I thought we might eat together, if you haven't any other plans . . . ? I've cooked for two.'

Paul turned away to slide his key into the lock of his front door. 'What's the occasion?' he asked.

Lucilla uttered a slightly nervous laugh. 'Does it have to be an occasion?'

'Just a neighbourly gesture, in fact?' he suggested dryly.

'Yes! Why not?'

He nodded. 'Give me five minutes to freshen up . . .' He was puzzled and suspicious, but he had no intention of rejecting the surprise invitation.

Lucilla struggled with a very natural nervousness as the surgeon strolled into her living room some minutes later. She smiled at him over her shoulder as she poured drinks. 'Whisky with a little water . . . is that right?'

'That's fine. You have an excellent memory.'

'Nurses are trained to remember details,' she reminded him. 'Do sit down, Paul. Make yourself at home. It's too early to eat, isn't it? I've made beef Stroganoff, by the way. I hope that's what you like?'

'Sounds great.' Taking his drink, Paul lowered his tall frame on to the cushions of the sofa, regarding her thoughtfully.

Lucilla felt a swooning excitement as she looked into those enigmatic dark eyes. She sat down beside him, putting her own untouched drink on the table. She wanted a clear head so that she couldn't blame anything that happened on too many Martinis. She was going into this with eyes wide open, throwing herself heart and soul at the man she loved, taking a desperate chance on the future.

'Now . . . tell me all about your game,' she invited brightly.

She sounded so much like a dutiful wife that a smile irresistibly twitched at Paul's mouth. He stifled the flicker of humour. For some reason that eluded him, she was all smiles, all encouragement, all warm and tempting invitation—and he didn't trust the sudden and bewildering change of heart.

'I think you'd be very bored if I took you at your word.' He leaned forward to set his glass on the table. As he sat back, he found that Lucilla had shifted position slightly so that she was suspiciously close to him. Her wafting perfume was delicate, titillating, but he refused to let it stir his senses. 'What's this all about, Lucilla?'

She widened her eyes. 'I don't know what you mean.' She reached for his glass. 'Let me top up your drink . . .'

Paul took the glass from her fingers in peremptory fashion and put it firmly on the table. 'Drinks, dinner for two, a new dress for my benefit—and don't tell me it isn't! I know women too well. Just what game are you playing?'

'It isn't a game, Paul. I'm very serious about this,' Lucilla said quietly, abandoning subterfuge. 'Everything's gone wrong and I'm trying to put it right. We started off on the wrong foot and things have gone from bad to worse. I can't believe you want this coldness between us any more than I do. That day on the cliffs . . .' She broke off, swamped by the memory of her anguish and anxiety.

'That day on the cliffs told me just how you feel about me,' he said harshly. 'Nothing's happened since to convince me that things have changed.'

She sighed. 'I knew it would be a waste of time trying to talk to you.'

'Then why bother?'

For answer, Lucilla reached to kiss him with lips that trembled only slightly at their temerity. There was no response. She hadn't expected it to be easy, she reminded herself as her heart sank. He was so proud. But he was also strongly sensual and surely the smouldering passion must soon surge, ignited by the flame of her own love and longing.

She kissed him again, lips lingering against the hard, unyielding mouth. His eyes were granite, his body rigid. She trailed butterfly kisses across his cheek and pressed her lips to the warm hollow in his throat where a pulse throbbed heavily. She slid an arm about his neck and pressed herself close to him, ignoring the continued resistance in his tall, tense frame.

'We've wasted so much time, Paul . . .' It was an aching, ardent murmur.

Silent, stony, Paul allowed her to kiss him, to twine

her fingers through his thick curls, to nestle against him in almost irresistible temptation. He wouldn't permit himself even the quiver of response while he doubted her sincerity.

His hands were clenched into fists, taut at his sides. Lucilla took one and gently prised open the long, clever fingers, then she curved them about the breast that ached so intensely for his touch. Sighing, she put her lips to the dark triangle of silky black hair that showed at the open neck of his thin shirt and spoke his name on a soft catch of her breath.

He frowned. 'You're making love to me, Lucilla.'

She nodded. 'I suppose I must be . . .' She smiled into his eyes in tender coaxing. 'Do you mind?' She slid her hand beneath his shirt to the warm, muscular chest and began to stroke him with light teasing fingers.

Paul was only human. Against his will, his body stirred, throbbed with fierce desire. 'You're playing with fire,' he warned in curt, clipped tones.

Lucilla bent her head to kiss the hand that cradled her soft breast. Paul's strong thumb moved across her sensitive flesh in a slow, sensuous caress that set her tingling, sweeping her with a tide of excitement that turned timorous, uncertain desire into real and devastating need.

'You don't know how much I want you,' she breathed on a half-sigh, half-sob of longing, unconsciously echoing words that had once been forced out of him by sheer, hungry passion.

Doubting her, distrusting her, Paul decided to put those words to the test. In one swift movement he thrust her back against the sofa cushions and took her startled face in both hands, covering her mouth with kisses that rendered her breathless. Lucilla clung to him, warm and weak and willing, and the need that had been so tensely controlled while she laid deliberate siege to his sensuality almost broke its bounds.

She was crushed by the weight of his heavy body as his hands moved over her, strong and sure, expert in arousal. His lips travelled hotly from tremulous mouth to pulsating throat and then to quickened breast, burning her flesh through the thin chiffon dress. She was swamped by his passion, her body melting in its sudden heat, her heart thundering to its heavy beat. She was afraid of the powerful force she had awakened even while her own excitement rushed to meet it headlong.

Straining to hold her even closer to him, her name a stifled groan, Paul kissed her again and again, parting her lips with the ardent hunger that had consumed him for so many frustrated days and nights, drinking deep of the sweetness of her mouth while the intoxicating perfume of her hair and skin quickened the urgency of his body's need.

Lucilla was all liquid fire, aflame with love and the ardent desire to give all, to hold nothing back, to belong to this man until the end of time. Didn't she love him with all her heart and soul and clamouring body?

Then, at the most intimate touch that was prelude to eagerly awaited ecstasy in Paul's embrace, she froze. With all her strength she pushed him away, suddenly finding that she couldn't give herself so completely to a man whose passion was urgent and ruthless—and utterly without love. Loving him just wasn't enough, after all. He had to love her too—and say so! He had said her name with longing, over and over again, as he held her, kissed and caressed her so persuasively, urging her towards surrender. The three vital words that she needed so much to hear seemed to be light years away from his lips—and his heart.

'*No*, I can't—I *can't*! I'm sorry!' She resisted him fiercely as he tried to take her back into his arms, to kiss her once more, refusing rejection. 'No, Paul! *Please!* Let me go—*I mean it!*' There was the hint of panic in her eyes and voice and in the way she broke free, leaping up to tug at her skirt and the bodice of her dress where eager, exploring hands had drawn it from shoulders and breasts.

Breathing hard, dark eyes glinting fiercely, Paul thrust furious fingers through wildly dishevelled black curls. 'What the devil are you trying to do to me?' He ground the words through clenched teeth. 'First it's all systems go—and then I mustn't touch you!'

'I didn't plan it that way—really I didn't,' Lucilla said desperately, eyes dark and wide with lingering desire and a trembling apprehension in the face of his fury.

His mouth curled with contempt. 'God knows what you planned! *I* don't! I just know that I'm always the loser in the games you play!' He got to his feet, trembling with anger and frustrated passion, knowing he must leave before he lost his head and took her by tempestuous force.

'I know you're cross . . .'

'*Cross!*' Paul's brows clamped together in a fierce ebony streak across his handsome features and he uttered a bleak and humourless laugh. 'You have a rare gift for understatement!'

'Furious, then,' she amended carefully. 'And disappointed . . .'

'Not for the first time where you're concerned. But it will certainly be the last, I promise you.' He moved towards the door on the grim, determined words.

Hurrying to him, Lucilla caught at his sleeve, forgetful of pride or anything but that she loved him. 'Don't go, Paul. *Please* don't go like this. Angry, hating me . . .' She swallowed a sob that welled in her throat, knowing that tears would irritate the naturally impatient surgeon.

He looked at her coldly. 'What is there to stay for? To have you blow hot and cold again so that a man doesn't know what to think—or to feel! No! I should have

known better than to trust a heartless, scheming slut
with your history and reputation! You're bad luck for
any man!' In two strides he reached the unit and seized
the photograph that he saw as a perpetual reminder of a
past love. He held it out accusingly, almost beside
himself with rage that he had given his heart to a girl who
was so unworthy of his love. 'What happened to *him*?
Did he find out what you were in time to save himself a
lot of heartache—but too late for the poor girl who was
married to him?' he demanded savagely.

Lucilla was so used to the startling resemblance between herself and her twin that she had looked at the
photograph a thousand times since Paul's first visit to her
flat and never once thought that it must have confirmed
his belief that she was the girl who had wrecked his
cousin's marriage.

Suddenly she was swept with a furious resentment that
he had never given her the benefit of the doubt and had
always been so ready to think badly of her. He had
judged her sight unseen, and nothing she'd said or done
since that first eventful day in Theatres had persuaded
him to change his mind, she thought bitterly.

'That isn't me,' she said icily. 'It's my sister.'

'Your sister!' Eyes narrowed, Paul looked more intently at the girl in the photograph and then at the girl
who confronted him with an angry blaze in her grey
eyes. They seemed to be one and the same . . . the sunny
smile, the warm and appealing prettiness, the confusion
of red-gold curls. 'You're incredibly alike,' he said
slowly, struggling with a sudden reversion of
preconceived ideas.

Lucilla fumed at the doubt in his deep voice. 'Twins
often are!' It was a sardonic flash of anger. '*That's*
Cilla—the girl you've always mistaken for me! Short for
Priscilla! I can't produce her to prove it because she's in
Australia. But I'm past caring about proving anything to

you! You're such an arrogant bastard! You only believe what you want to believe and see what you want to see! And you're always right, aren't you? Well, this time you were *so* wrong! About me—about everything!'

'It seems that way.' Paul was stunned and shaken, needing time to reassess his thoughts and feelings about this girl who had invaded and won total possession of his heart despite the barriers set up by the mind that had rigidly refused to accept that he had confused her with someone else.

But how could he possibly have known that Lucilla was a twin?

CHAPTER FOURTEEN

'*SEEMS!*' Lucilla echoed stormily. 'You still don't believe it, do you?'

'It's a very convenient moment to claim the existence of a twin sister!' Paul said dryly.

Her hands clenched. She was so angry she could have struck him. But that wouldn't solve anything. 'What do you want—birth certificates?'

'I know I sound sceptical. Okay, so you've an identical twin. But I'm not convinced that Greg Harman left Pam for your sister and not you,' he told her tautly. Perhaps it was unreasonable and unfair, but he had to be sure. He loved Lucilla, no matter what, but that tiny niggle of doubt would torment him for ever if he didn't make sure it was completely banished.

Lucilla glowered. 'He married Cilla! Is that convincing enough for you?'

'Married her!' It was totally unexpected news to Paul.

'And took her to Australia with him. I had a letter from her last week, if you'd like to see it!'

He shook his head. 'You had plenty of opportunity to tell me that Greg had married again—and to mention your sister,' he said stiffly, still puzzled.

'Oh, I *tried*! Believe me, I tried!' Lucilla said bitterly. 'When did you ever have the time or the patience to listen, to take an interest in anything *I* said or did —except when the mood took you and you thought you only had to lift a finger and I'd fall into your arms! A girl with *my* history and *my* reputation!' She threw the words at him on a spurt of renewed hurt and fury. 'But you had the wrong girl!'

Paul looked down at her pale, furious face and saw the unhappiness behind the anger in her lovely eyes, the betraying tremble of her small chin as she fought back the tears. His heart suddenly smote him. It had been an understandable confusion compounded by misunderstandings and a series of quarrels, but he didn't doubt that loving Lucilla had always been his destiny—and, now that he was no longer blinded by the prejudice of the past, he saw very clearly that she might have loved him if he had treated her differently. So he couldn't allow the chance of possible happiness in the future to be totally shattered by the angry words and actions of the present.

'A bad case of mistaken identity,' he said with a sudden smile of particular charm. 'I agree with your diagnosis, Sister Flint. What's the prognosis, in your view? I think it's a suitable case for the right kind of treatment, don't you?' It was apology and regret and a plea for forgiveness all in one, his deep voice warm with special meaning. Tilting her chin with gentle fingers, he bent his head to kiss her.

Lucilla jerked away before his mouth could claim her own, angry and astonished at the cool conceit of the man. Not one word of apology for the mistake that had created a wall of hate and hostility between them before he ever set eyes on her! Not one word of regret for having misjudged and hurt and quarrelled with her all these weeks! He thought he could forget everything and make light love to her as if nothing had happened!

'Don't you dare!' she flared, a tempest raging so fiercely in her breast that it temporarily deadened all feeling for him. 'Don't ever try to kiss me or lay a finger on me again! I wish it was possible never to see or speak to you again!'

'You don't mean that, you know,' Paul said quietly, sure that the passionate outburst had its roots in something more than resentment. He had hurt her so much more than he knew, but he took comfort from the memory of the way she had clung, kissed him, responded to his lovemaking. She could be persuaded to forgive him eventually, he felt.

'Every word of it!' He was so infuriatingly confident that he knew how she felt better than she did!

'We've had some good moments, Lucilla. There could be so many more.'

She stared at him. 'Good moments? When? You've never liked me and we've fought almost constantly since the first day you came to the General!' Whisking the photograph from his hand, she crossed the room in a fury to return it to its shelf.

'Oh, Lucy . . .' The small, soft name vibrated with longing. He saw her stiffen. Moving swiftly to her side, Paul put a hand along her cheek in a tender, tentative caress. 'I was fighting what you were doing to me,' he told her, low and urgent. 'I've wanted you from the first moment I saw you . . .'

She flung off his hand. 'For all the wrong reasons —and I'm supposed to like you for it? I don't! I hate your arrogance! I hate you too!' It was almost true in that moment when desire for her throbbed in his deep voice and glowed in his dark eyes and warmed that very special smile, and she despised him for it. That was all she would ever be to him, she thought bitterly—a potential bedmate! She was good enough to satisfy the sexual hunger of a sensual, too sure of himself surgeon but not good enough to love and cherish and need for the rest of his life!

Paul looked down at the angry girl with understanding and a wealth of love that she was in no mood to recognise. He found it hard to be patient when he needed her in his arms, in his heart and at his side throughout all the years to come.

'You don't know what you're saying,' he told her firmly, unconsciously autocratic. 'You're too emotional to be rational or to listen to anything I have to say, I'm afraid. I'll forgo the beef Stroganoff and leave you to calm down. We'll talk tomorrow.'

'You can forgo everything as far as I'm concerned!' Lucilla was irritated by that cool assumption that she would meekly fall in with anything he suggested once her temper had cooled. 'Just get out of my flat right now, and stay out of my life for good!'

The exasperation of a man fast losing patience with a stubborn and independent girl flickered across Paul's handsome features. 'If that's really the way you want it . . . !'

'It is!'

Paul shrugged his broad shoulders and strode from the room in an ominous silence. Lucilla stood very still, rigid with anger and dismay and the terrible dread that he would take her at her word, until the snap of the outer door broke the spell. Then she sank to the floor and put her head on the sofa cushions and wept.

Loving an arrogant, unfeeling surgeon had turned out to be an absolute disaster, just as she had feared from the start—and her heart was the major casualty.

She found it hard to believe that a whole day could pass without sight or sound of Paul. So much for his assurance that he would be in touch! She knew he had been in his flat for some part of the day, for he had played Rachmaninov, very loudly, the furious rise and fall of the recorded music obviously reflecting his mood. Hearing the music through the thin dividing wall, her heart throbbing and sobbing in sympathy, Lucilla had been reminded of the tumultuous passion that had nearly swept her into surrender. The ache for him was overwhelming, but she had firmly resisted the temptation to

go to him and throw herself into his arms all over again.
He must make the first move! He owed her that much, at
least!

'Looking for me, lovely?'

Lucilla spun, heart leaping with wild hope, at the light
tap on her shoulder. She'd been craning for a sight of just
one person in the crowd that thronged the harbour
instead of watching the race that was in full swing, gay
procession of brightly decorated boats bobbing and
plunging to the shouts and cheers and whistles of the
delighted spectators.

'Oh, Laurie . . . !' With an effort, she kept the painful
surge of disappointment from showing in her smile.

'How's it going?'

'Pretty well, I think. They're still afloat, anyway.'
Lucilla pretended enthusiastic support for her friends as
the small fishing-boat veered in all directions, but her
spirits were as overcast as the sky that Sunday.

'How come a pretty girl like you is all by herself in this
crowd?' Laurie demanded lightly.

'Because I'm the only one with sense enough to stay
on shore, I expect!'

He laughed. 'What about me? I opted out too.'

'Then you can keep me company for the rest of the
race—and join your cheers to mine.'

'I can't think of a nicer way to spend the rest of the day
than keeping you company,' he assured her promptly,
smiling at her with warm friendliness.

Making his way through the crush to be in position for
the arrival of Sally Lloyd's splendid launch, well in the
lead as its crew paddled furiously with the toy swords
that matched their piratical get-up, Paul came to a
sudden halt as he saw the laughing, lighthearted Theatre
Sister with Laurie Jesmond's arm draped about her slim
shoulders. His eyes hardened abruptly. So did his heart.

It wasn't easy for a proud man like himself to swallow

some of the things that Lucilla had said, however well deserved. Paul had spent the intervening hours in coming to terms with his pride and admitting that he wanted her at all costs and deciding that an entirely new beginning was essential to their relationship. They both needed time to reflect on how they really felt about each other, he felt—and the weekend would provide an interval between old and new attitude. Now, seeing how happily she was spending her day with another man, Paul doubted that she cared anything at all for him.

The hair on her nape inexplicably prickling and all her finely-tuned senses quickening, Lucilla turned her head to look into the surgeon's glowering eyes. Her heart flew up into her throat and she could scarcely breathe for the suffocating pound of her heart as she realised the frost behind that smouldering gaze.

They looked at each other for a long, long moment. Then Lucilla turned back and joined with Laurie in shouting support for the small boat that was somehow managing to catch up with the leading launch. There was a burn in her breast and the sting of tears behind her eyes, but she cheered with the best rather than let Paul see that anguish of mind and heart.

About to stride on, to put a determined distance between them, Paul was thrust forward by a good-natured surge of people anxious for a better view of the race. Against his wish and his will, he found himself at Lucilla's side.

The girl in the mint-green linen dress that complemented her warm colouring scarcely glanced at him, apparently more interested in the exciting conclusion of the harbour race. It was Laurie who welcomed him, obviously assuming that he had made his way through the crowd to join them.

'Hallo, Savidge. Going great guns, isn't it?' he enthused. 'I suppose you're supporting the Lloyd boat and

Evan? Spare a cheer for our boat, won't you? I really think they're going to make it . . .'

A shout of alarm cut across the words and there was a sickening crunch as launch and fishing-boat collided. The turning tide had caused a surge that swept the smaller boat off course and into the side of the launch. Inevitably, it came off worse, its prow shattered by the impact.

There was a loud groan of disappointment from those who would have liked to see the smaller boat complete the course if it didn't actually succeed in its brave attempt to beat the launch to the finishing-post.

As the boat began to fill with water and list ominously, Keith and his crew hastily abandoned ship, swimming for the jetty that stretched like a long finger into the harbour at that point, the heavy frock-coats of pseudo-Victorian doctors and the voluminous skirts and flowing veils of pseudo-Victorian nurses hampering their progress. The boat appeared to be the only casualty.

'Evan's been hurt!' exclaimed Lucilla.

'What? Where . . . ?' Paul followed her pointing finger with searching gaze, alerted by the alarm in her voice.

Evan had been leaning precariously over the side of the launch, spurred on to greater efforts by the cheerful rivalry of his friends in the pursuing boat and the excited shouts of the crowd, ploughing his pirate's sword through the waves with both hands.

Watching him, Lucilla had wondered if he was too intent on the race to notice the surge of the tide or to realise the danger as Keith's boat swung inwards on a huge wave. As it rammed the launch, the prow had struck Evan and toppled him into the water.

'He went in when the boats collided,' she said anxiously. 'I think . . . I'm sure he hit his head! He ought to have surfaced by now, but I can't see him anywhere . . .'

'I can . . . !' Paul forced a way through the crowd and raced along the jetty, stripping off his coat as he ran, and dived into the sea as close as he could get to the unconscious man. Evan was just going under again as Paul reached him, grabbing for his shoulders. He supported his friend, keeping his head clear of the water and forcing air into the flooded lungs, until a dinghy manned by volunteer lifeguards could steer a passage through the flotilla of finishing vessels.

It had been one of those freak accidents that people witness without realising its seriousness. Keith and his crew were certainly unaware that Evan was in danger of drowning as they swam for shore, shouting and waving to each other, although they had seen him plunge overboard at the moment of collision. People in the crowd had seen the incident but dismissed it as Sally Lloyd's launch continued a clear winner towards the finishing post, virtually unscathed. In all the excitement, not one of the crew realised that Evan was missing.

Evan was scooped to safety and Paul hauled in after him, and the dinghy headed at full speed for the point where a First Aid post was manned by members of the St John Ambulance Brigade.

With her heart in her mouth, Lucilla fought her way through the milling throng, elbowing people aside and almost crying with frustration when they unwittingly blocked her path. Laurie was close on her heels.

By the time they reached the post, Evan had been lifted from the dinghy to a stretcher and was on his way to a waiting ambulance, covered in blankets, his fair hair darkened by sea-water and blood. As she saw the blue, pinched look of his good-looking features, Lucilla's heart briefly stopped . . . then plunged with relief as she saw that he was breathing.

Still coughing up some of the sea-water he'd swallowed in the struggle to keep his heavily-built friend afloat, Paul stood on the quayside, water dripping from his hair and his sodden clothes.

Lucilla ran to him and clutched at his wet sleeve. 'Is he . . . oh, how is he?' she blurted breathlessly.

'He'll do.' Paul had checked Evan over as best he could in the dinghy and satisfied himself that he was in no danger. 'He's got a nasty cut on his head and he's concussed and he's inhaled a lot of water, but he'll recover.' He covered her hand in a fierce, bruising grip. 'There's no real cause for concern,' he added reassuringly, seeing her pallor and distress. Was Evan much more important to her than he could ever hope to be—and had his friend's near-death from drowning brought it home to her? he wondered.

Sick with relief, Lucilla could still thrill to his touch, to the warmth in his deep voice. She was aflame with admiration for him too. 'Paul, you were fantastic! I didn't know anyone could move that fast! You saved Evan's life!'

'Don't make a fuss, Lucy,' he said brusquely, aware of stares and pointing fingers, huddles of excited observers, smiles and nods and shouts of approval from strangers who had seen the rescue. Paul hated public display and he disliked being the centre of so much attention. 'Someone else would have fished him out if I hadn't. There were enough people to see that he was in trouble. Don't try to turn me into a hero, for God's sake!'

Lucilla smiled at him warmly, knowing now that he was at his most impatient when he was most moved. She had come to know him so well during the weeks that she had learned to love him so deeply.

'It was bloody well done, anyway,' Laurie approved warmly, slapping the surgeon on the back.

An ambulance-man draped a blanket about Paul's wet shoulders. 'We'll take you in with us, sir. Get you dried off and checked out . . .'

Paul nodded. 'Right you are!' Releasing his hold on
Lucilla, he turned towards the vehicle. 'But I'm afraid I
shall drip all over the floor,' he warned with his slow,
attractive smile.

'We won't worry about that, sir. We're used to worse.'

After urging Laurie to find her friends and tell them
she'd gone to the General, Lucilla hurried after them.
Paul got into the ambulance and immediately reached
for Evan's limp wrist to check his pulse, seeing that his
breathing was laboured and stertorous.

'It's all right, I am a doctor,' Paul said firmly as the
paramedic who was about to place an oxygen mask in
position opened his mouth to protest.

Lucilla spoke to the driver. 'I'd like to come with you.'

'Are you a relative, miss?' He looked at her doubtfully.

'No, just a friend. But . . .'

'Don't worry, miss. We'll look after him for you,' he
assured her with brisk kindliness. 'You follow in your
own transport and they'll let you see him at the hospital.'

'Sister Flint works at the General,' Paul interposed,
seeing the continued anxiety in Lucilla's expression and
knowing what she must be feeling. 'So does your patient,
by the way.'

'Oh, in that case . . . in you get, Sister!' The driver
gave her a hand up the step and then shut the doors.

The ambulance made good progress through the narrow streets of Camsea and the outer area of Camhurst to
the General while three pairs of eyes watched vigilantly
for some sign of returning consciousness in the patient.
Lucilla was glad of Paul's silent presence, the comforting
clasp of his hand and the reassuring smile in his eyes
whenever she glanced at him. Within a mile of their
destination came the first looked-for change in Evan's
breathing and a flicker of eyelids that brought Paul
swiftly to his feet to examine the pupils.

'Coming round,' he said thankfully.

Lucilla felt she could relax at last, Evan was going to be fine except for a bruise and a nasty headache, she decided. Within a couple of days he'd be sitting up and making light of the whole thing and flirting with any pretty nurse who crossed his path. Dear, predictable, goodnatured Evan! She was very, very fond of him. But even the dreadful anxiety about him hadn't shocked her heart into supposing he was her real love.

Anxious for Evan, she had been much more anxious for Paul as he struggled in the sea with his heavy burden, at risk from the number of carnival-clad competitors who brandished a variety of odd-shaped paddles in their attempts to get to the finishing post, regardless of anything in their way and apparently unaware of the drama taking place under their very noses. Lucilla had been terrified that a carelessly wielded cricket bat or lump of wood or frying pan or other strange object might whack Paul across the head and put *his* life at risk.

She wouldn't want to live without Paul.

Spoken aloud, it would seem unnecessarily dramatic, even absurd. The silent utterance of her heart was totally convincing. She loved him, so much, more than anything in the world. Her stubborn pride dissolved in the flame of love and need and she knew she must reach out to secure her happiness.

Lucilla was sure, deep down, that Paul was very close to caring for her too. It showed in his touch, in his warm glance, in his concern for her anxiety about Evan—a misunderstood anxiety, she realised, determined to put him right on that point as soon as possible. And it showed in the very special smile he gave her as he helped her down from the ambulance on arrival.

A & E had been alerted en route and Evan was hurried into a cubicle by waiting staff. After a brief consultation with Paul and the paramedic, the duty Casualty Officer went to examine the surgeon, who was one of their own and very popular.

Paul was immediately surrounded by nurses who wanted to know the details of the accident and his part in it. He was unexpectedly patient with their eager questions, but it was obvious to Lucilla that a naturally modest man would prefer to slip away and never mention the matter again.

She regarded him with a smile in her eyes. His still-damp hair clustered in tight black curls and the thin shirt clung damply, dark chest hair showing through, muscles rippling strongly in back and shoulders. That powerful physique had undoubtedly been an asset to him that afternoon. He had discarded the red blanket and removed sodden shoes and socks, and the sight of strong bare feet on the polished floor caught at Lucilla's heart.

He looked so human, so vulnerable, stripped of his rather forbidding dignity and that austere arrogance as he stood in wet clothes and bare feet in the midst of excited young nurses, answering their questions with smiling patience and a kindliness that showed Lucilla another and surprising side to his nature. There was so much more to Paul than she'd known when she fell irrevocably in love with him, she admitted, on a surge of wonder that her heart had known long before her head that the new SSO was a man to trust with her happiness.

They had both leaped to hasty, ill-founded conclusions about each other, but fortunately no lasting damage had been done. It must be possible to salvage a promise for the future from the debris of mistakes and misunderstandings.

In the meantime, Lucilla went to his rescue. 'Come along, nurses. You must have work to do and Mr Savidge should be changing into dry clothes.' As the nurses melted away before the brisk authority of Sister Theatres, Lucilla turned to the surgeon with a very unprofessional smile for him, glowing, golden, brimming with love. 'I'm afraid you *are* a hero whether you like it or not.'

'To the juniors.'

'Not only the juniors, Paul,' she said quietly, with unmistakable meaning.

Paul searched the lovely face for proof of the love that shone in her eyes and trembled in her lilting voice. 'I'd like to believe that doing a favour for a friend has encouraged you to think of me as someone special,' he told her, smiling.

Lucilla's heart shook. 'You've always been special to me, Paul,' she said simply. 'Even when you were being so beastly to me.'

'If this is one of your games . . .' Paul began with a dangerous edge to his voice and a suspicious glint in his dark eyes.

'When will you believe I don't play at love?' She was almost impatient with his doubts.

'Are you saying you love *me*?' It was brusque, scarcely encouraging. But he wanted so much to believe that she cared . . . if only a little. For, given time and the right treatment, it might be a case of lasting mutual love.

Lucilla sighed. 'You don't make it easy for a girl, do you?' Then, without a care for their clinical surroundings or the startled eyes of colleagues and patients, she reached to kiss him with her loving heart on her lips.

It wasn't expected or acceptable behaviour for surgeon or Sister, but Paul caught her close, crushing her to him, his heart hammering so fiercely that she felt its pound against her own tumultuous breast.

'You've never made it easy for me,' he told her in savage tones. 'But it didn't stop me loving you. You'd better mean what you're saying and doing this time, because you're likely to end up married to me, Sister!'

Before Lucilla could assure him that she couldn't

think of anything she wanted more passionately than to
be his wife, Paul took possession of her mouth in a way
that warned her that he would be a very demanding and
autocratic and impatient husband . . .

NOW ON VIDEO

Two great Romances available on video . . .*
from leading video retailers for just

£9·99
R.R.P.

The love you find in Dreams.

'from Autumn 1987

Doctor Nurse Romances

Romance in modern medical life

Read more about the lives and loves of doctors and nurses in the fascinatingly different backgrounds of contemporary medicine. These are the three Doctor Nurse romances to look out for next month.

INVISIBLE DOCTOR
Holly North

VALENTINES FOR NURSE CLEO
Lilian Darcy

NURSE ON THE MOVE
Frances Crowne

Buy them from your usual paperback stockist, or write to: Mills & Boon Reader Service, P.O. Box 236, Thornton Rd, Croydon, Surrey CR9 3RU, England. Readers in Southern Africa — write to: Independent Book Services Pty, Postbag X3010, Randburg, 2125, S. Africa.

Mills & Boon
the rose of romance

Bestselling Author Carole Mortimer's latest title 'WITCHCHILD'

A heart-rending tale of break-up and reconciliation. Millionaire 'Hawk' Sinclair mistakenly accuses novelist Leonie Spencer of ruthlessly pursuing his son Hal for a share in the family fortune.

It's actually a case of mistaken identity, but as a consequence the bewitching Leonie finds herself caught up in a maelstrom of passion, blackmail and kidnap.

Available November 1987 Price: £2.95

W🌐RLDWIDE

From Boots, Martins, John Menzies, W H Smith, Woolworths and other paperback stockists.